JAKE MADDOX
GRAPHIC NOVELS

HALF-PIPE PANIC

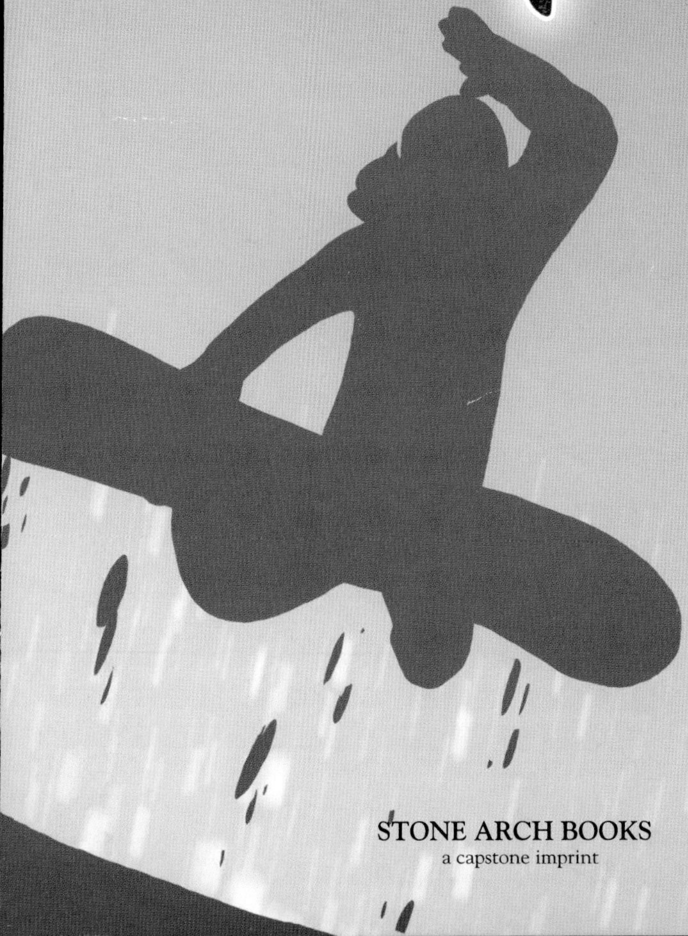

STONE ARCH BOOKS
a capstone imprint

JAKE MADDOX
GRAPHIC NOVELS

Jake Maddox Graphic Novels are published by
Stone Arch Books, a Capstone imprint
1710 Roe Crest Drive
North Mankato, Minnesota 56003

www.mycapstone.com

Library of Congress Cataloging-in-Publication Data
is available on the Library of Congress website.

ISBN: 978-1-4965-6044-5 (library binding)
ISBN: 978-1-4965-6048-3 (paperback)
ISBN: 978-1-4965-6052-0 (ebook PDF)

Summary: Payton Park is an artist on a snowboard.
He's wowed many fans with his incredible half-pipe
tricks. But after an epic wipeout, he's humiliated
when a video of it shows up on the internet for all to
see. Now the embarrassing moment keeps replaying
in his mind and facing the half-pipe fills him with
dread. Can Park shake off his fears and regain his
confidence in time to challenge his biggest rival at
the next big event?

Editor: Aaron Sautter
Designer: Brann Garvey
Production: Laura Manthe

Printed in the United States of America.
010836S18

HALF-PIPE PANIC

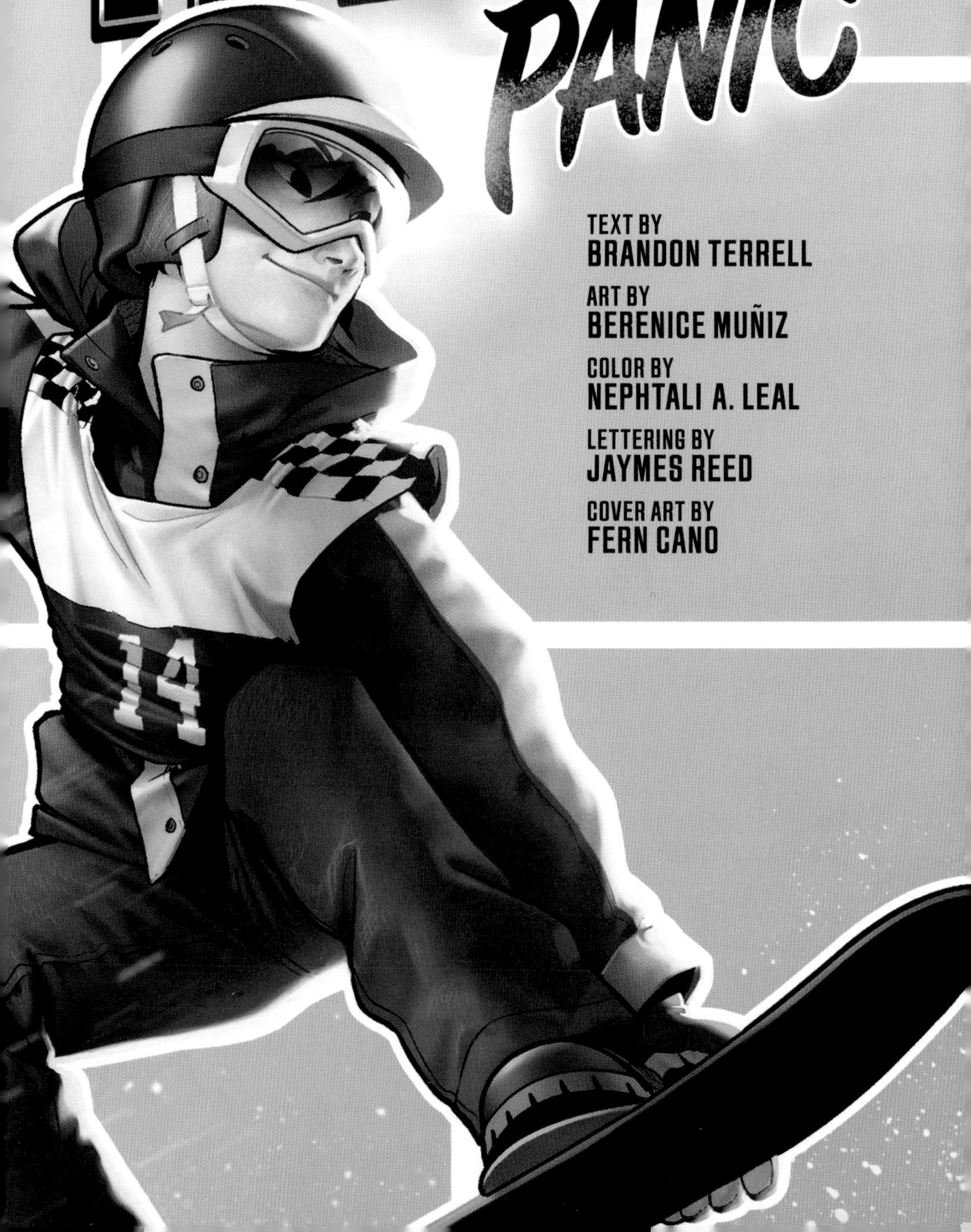

14

TEXT BY
BRANDON TERRELL

ART BY
BERENICE MUÑIZ

COLOR BY
NEPHTALI A. LEAL

LETTERING BY
JAYMES REED

COVER ART BY
FERN CANO

CAST OF CHARACTERS

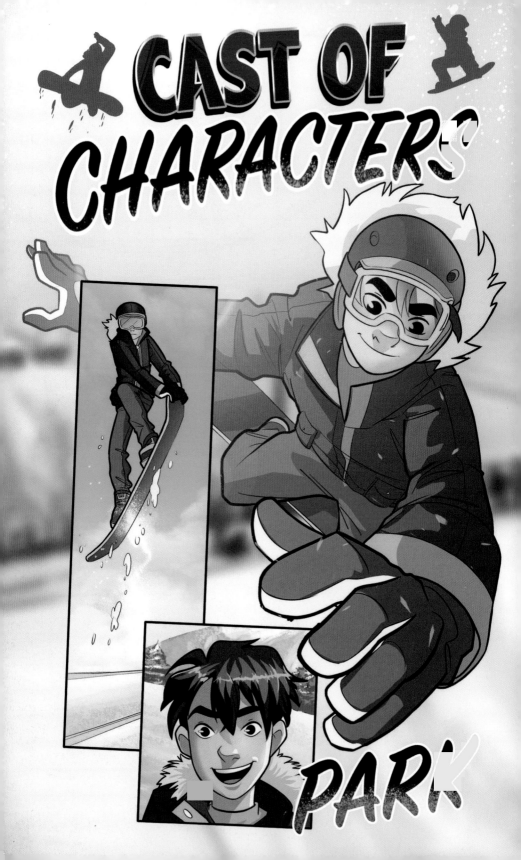

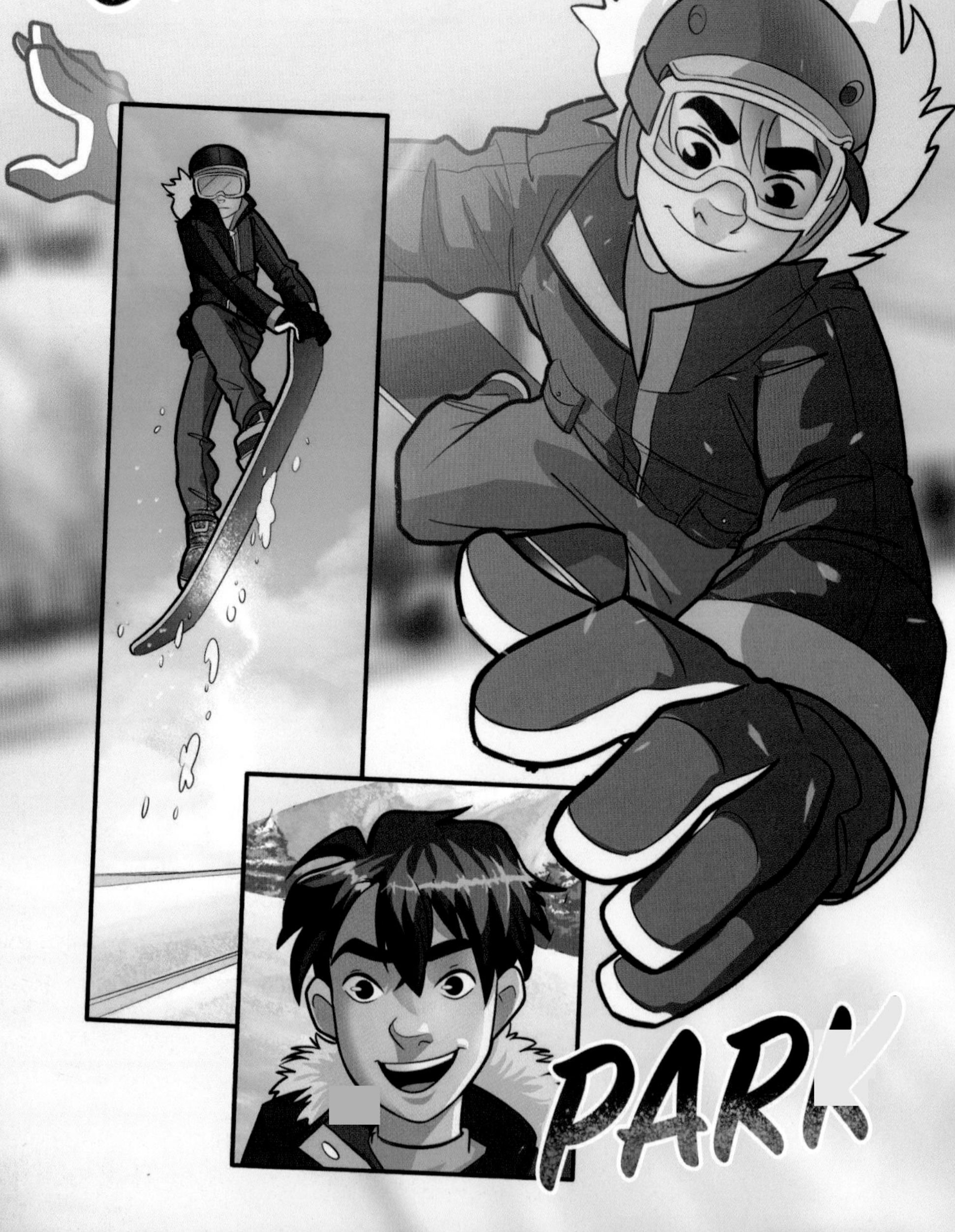
PARK

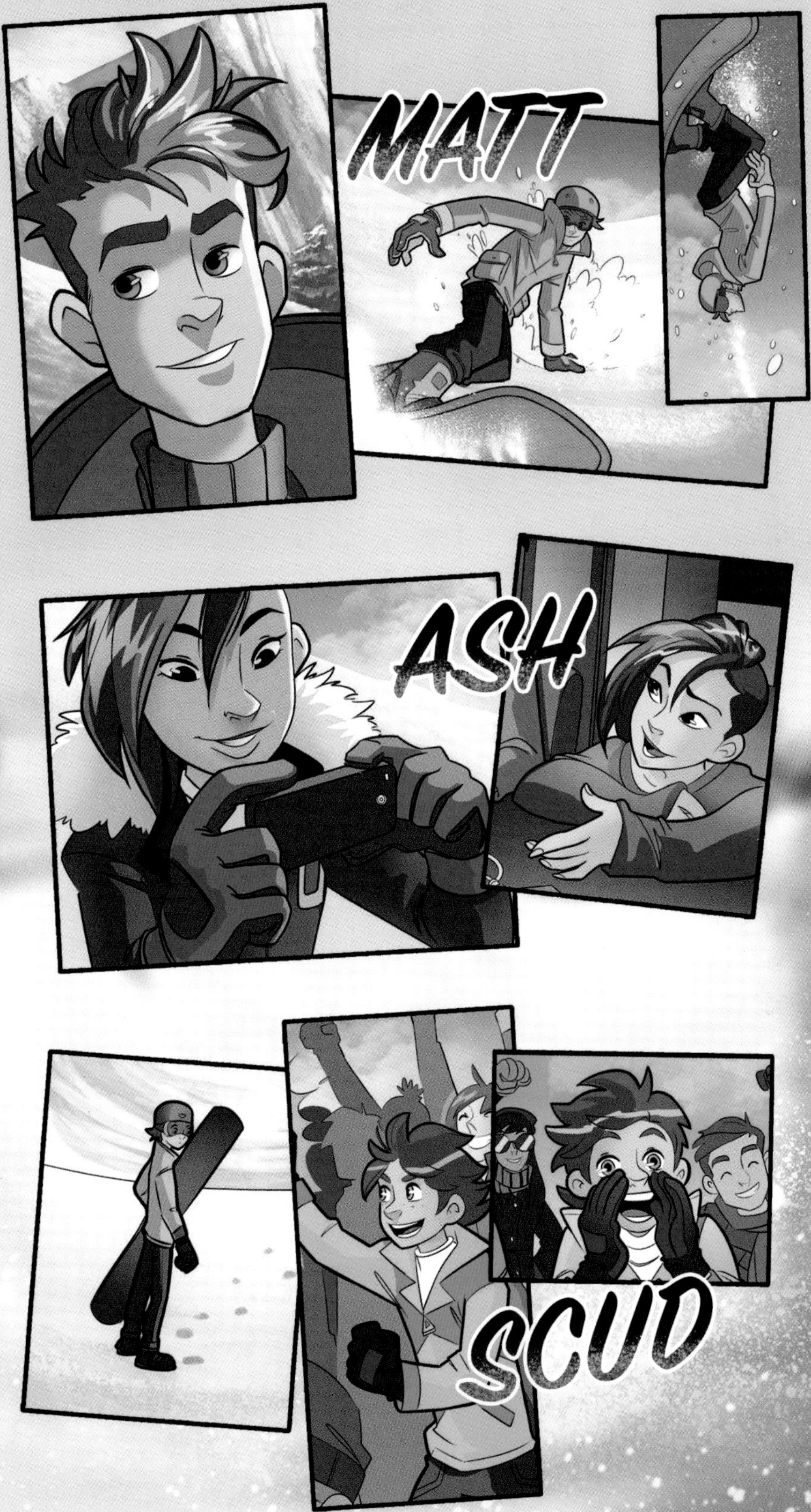
MATT
ASH
SCUD

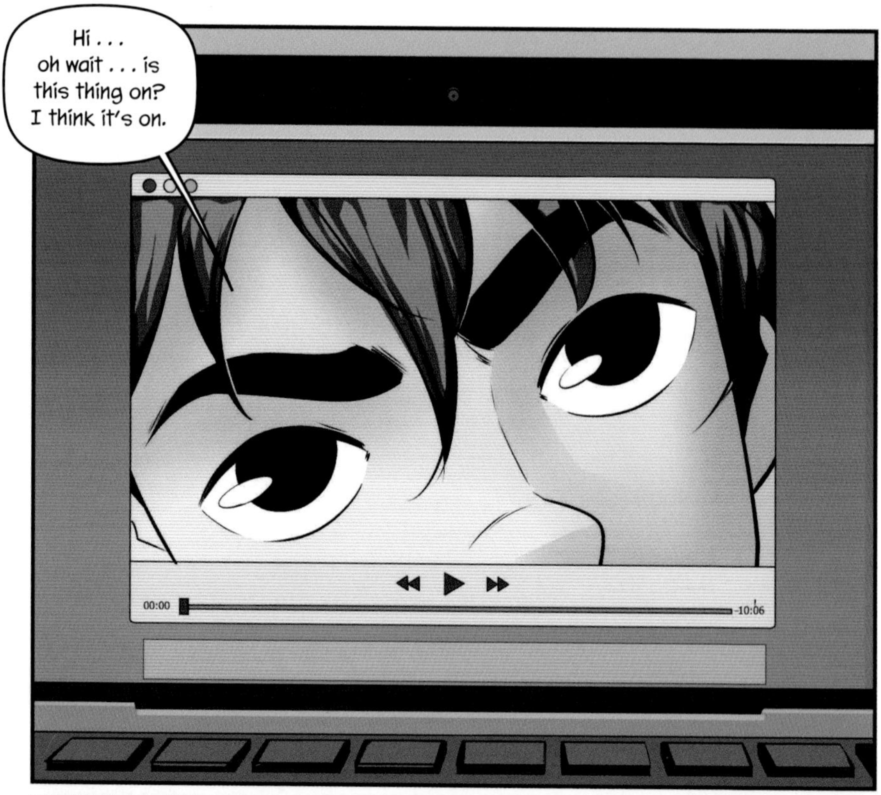

Hi . . .
oh wait . . . is this thing on? I think it's on.
00:00
-10:06

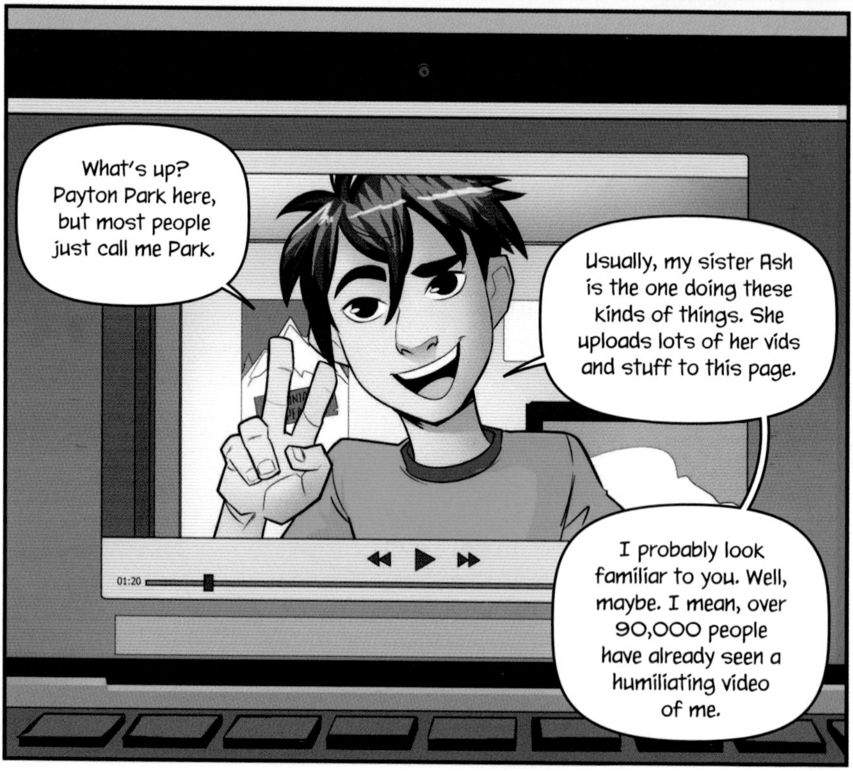

What's up? Payton Park here, but most people just call me Park.
Usually, my sister Ash is the one doing these kinds of things. She uploads lots of her vids and stuff to this page.
I probably look familiar to you. Well, maybe. I mean, over 90,000 people have already seen a humiliating video of me.
01:20

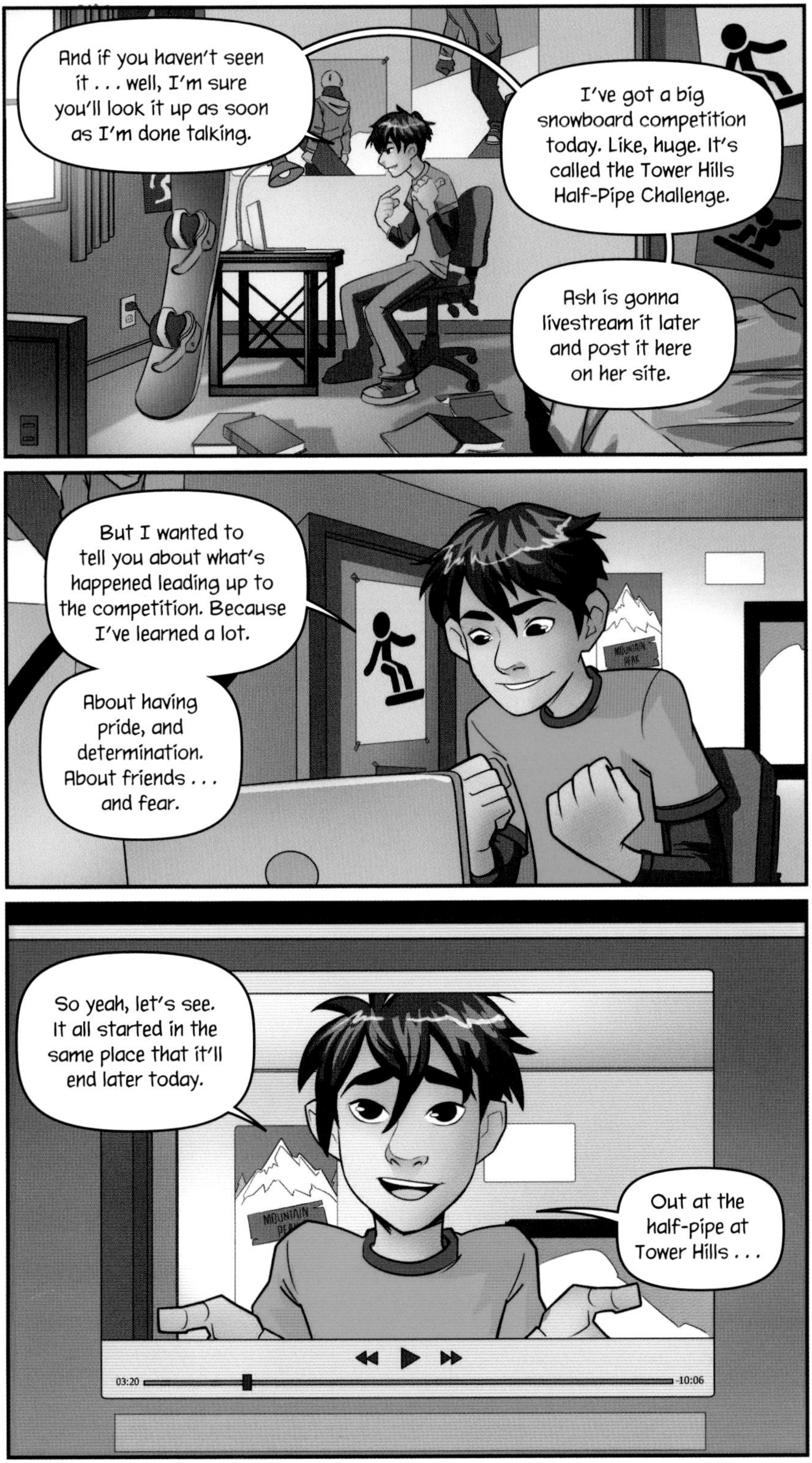

And if you haven't seen it . . . well, I'm sure you'll look it up as soon as I'm done talking.
I've got a big snowboard competition today. Like, huge. It's called the Tower Hills Half-Pipe Challenge.
Ash is gonna livestream it later and post it here on her site.
But I wanted to tell you about what's happened leading up to the competition. Because I've learned a lot.
About having pride, and determination. About friends . . . and fear.
So yeah, let's see. It all started in the same place that it'll end later today.
Out at the half-pipe at Tower Hills . . .
03:20
-10:06

8

9

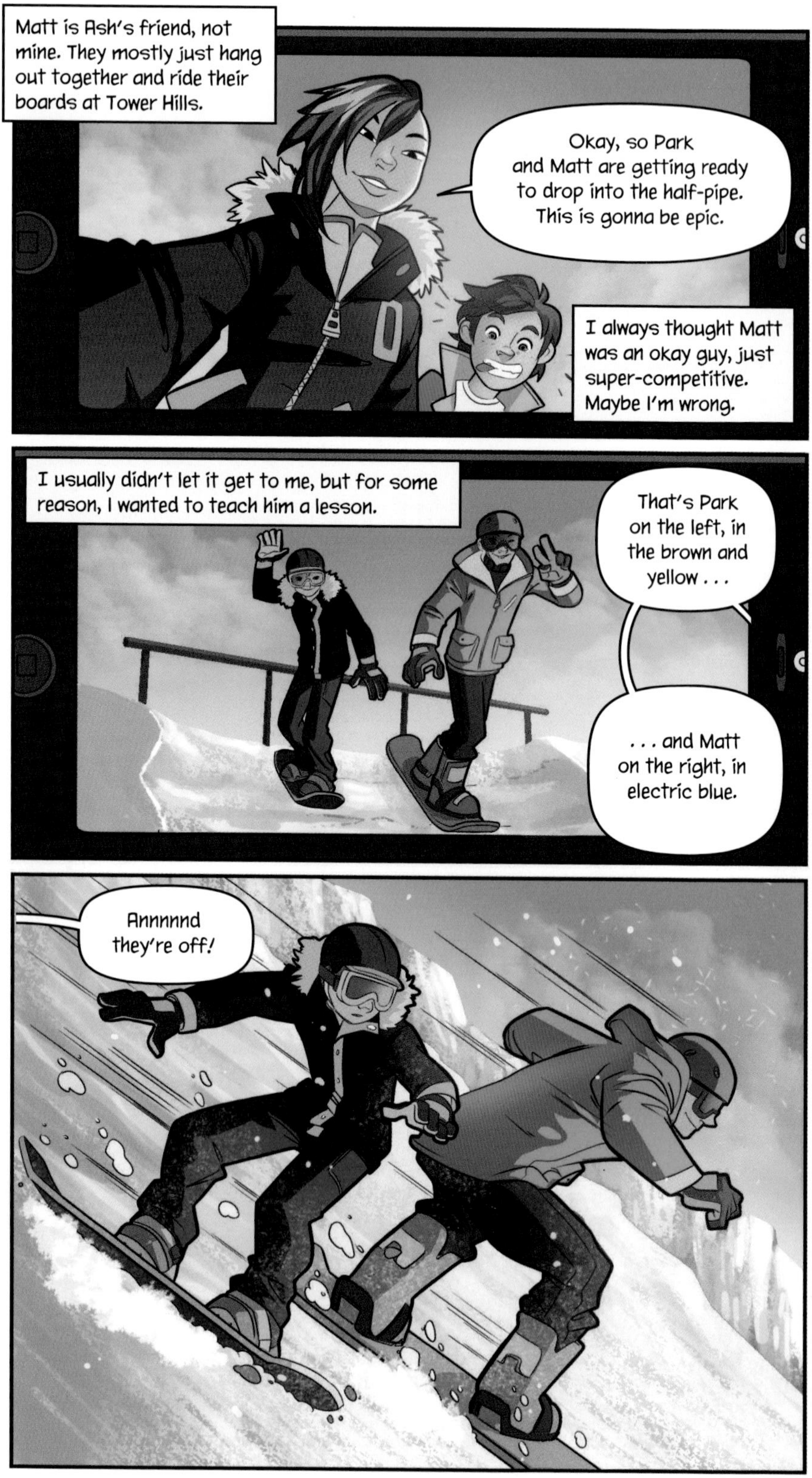
Matt is Ash's friend, not mine. They mostly just hang out together and ride their boards at Tower Hills.
Okay, so Park and Matt are getting ready to drop into the half-pipe. This is gonna be epic.
I always thought Matt was an okay guy, just super-competitive. Maybe I'm wrong.
I usually didn't let it get to me, but for some reason, I wanted to teach him a lesson.
That's Park on the left, in the brown and yellow . . .
. . . and Matt on the right, in electric blue.
Annnnnd they're off!

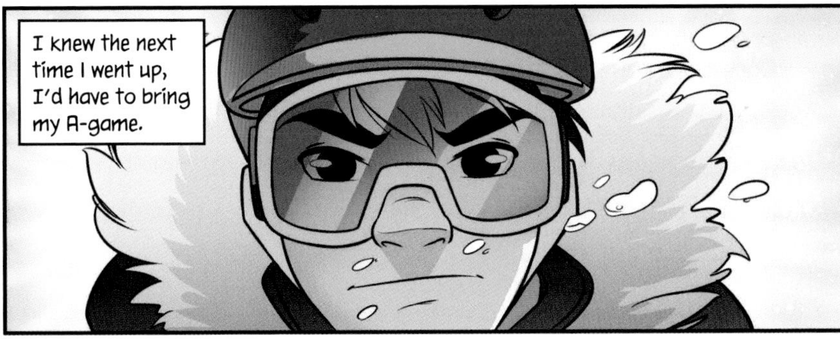
I knew the next time I went up, I'd have to bring my A-game.

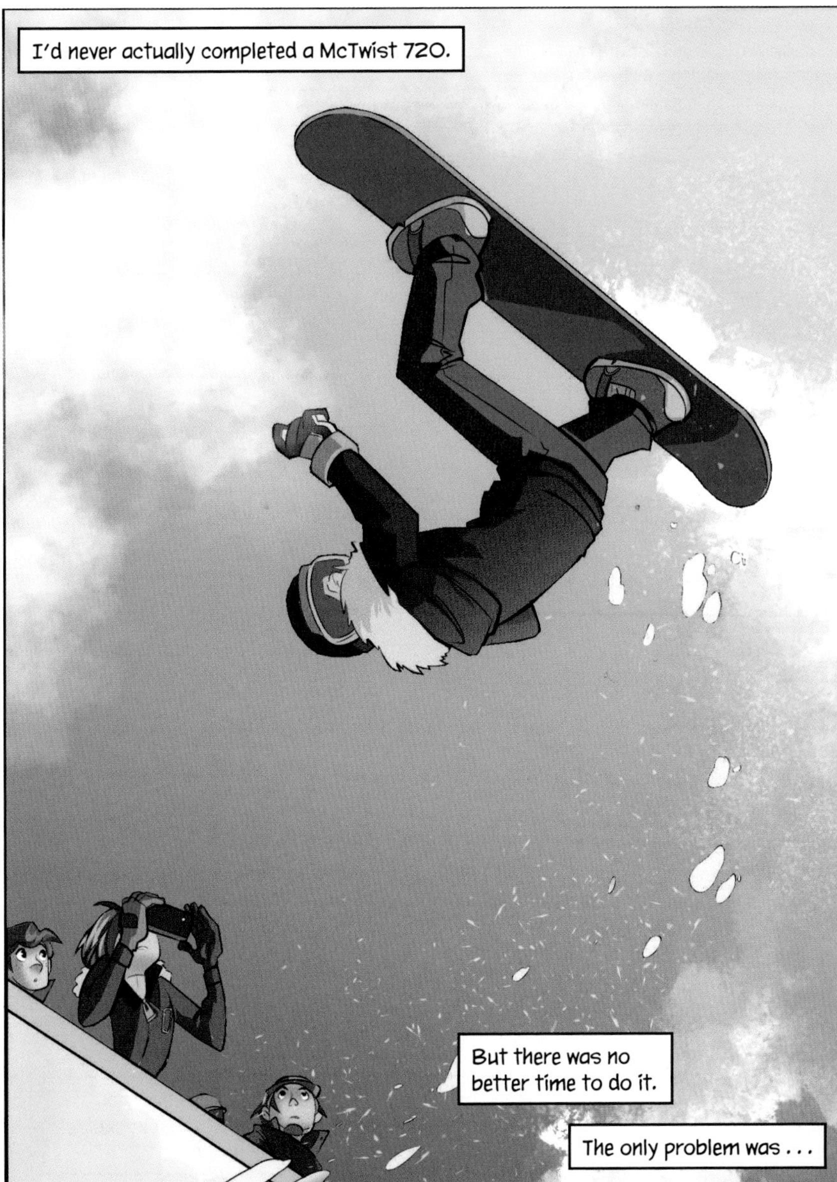
I'd never actually completed a McTwist 720.
But there was no better time to do it.
The only problem was . . .

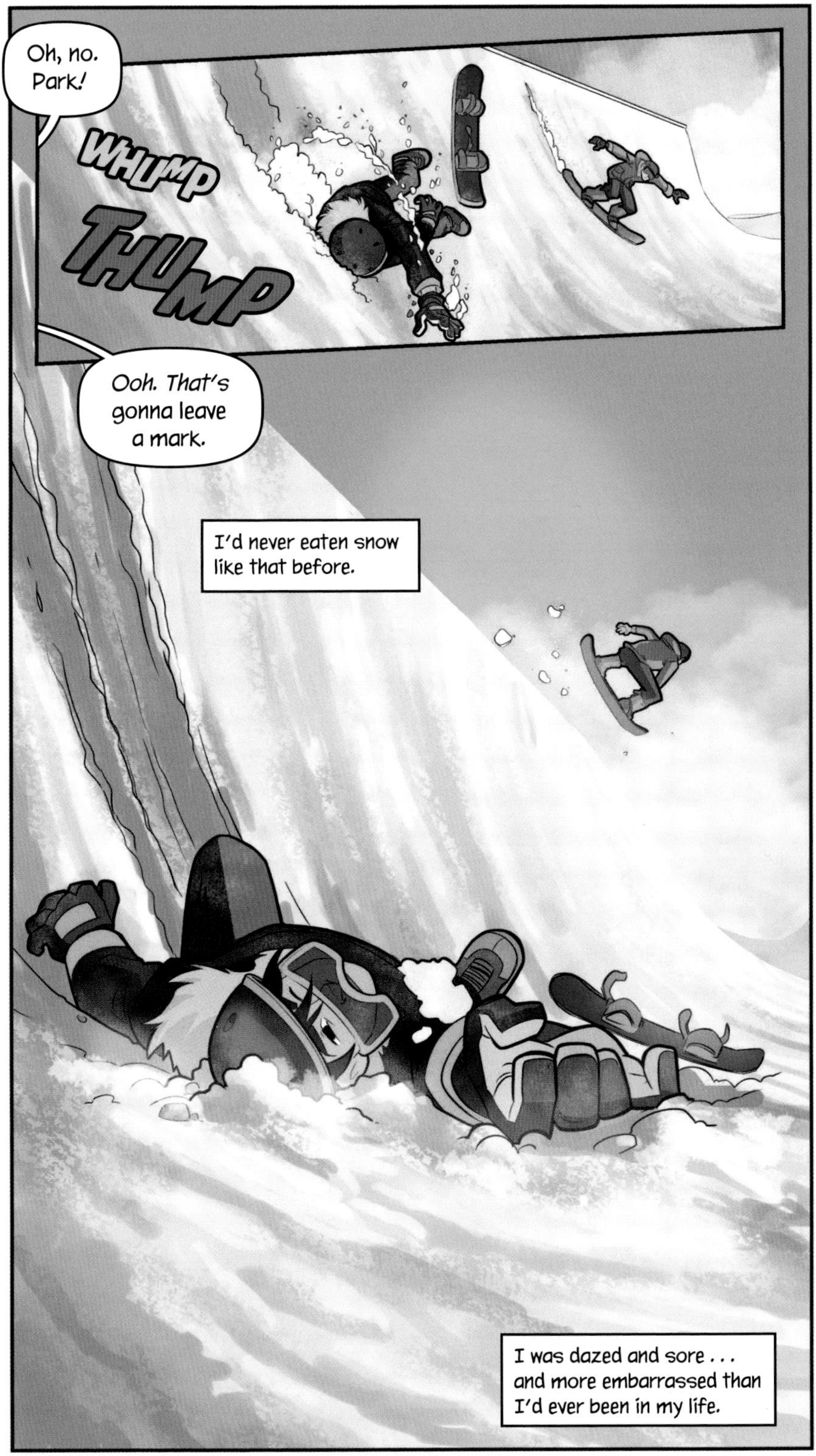

Oh, no. Park!
WHUMP
THUMP
Ooh. That's gonna leave a mark.
I'd never eaten snow like that before.
I was dazed and sore . . . and more embarrassed than I'd ever been in my life.

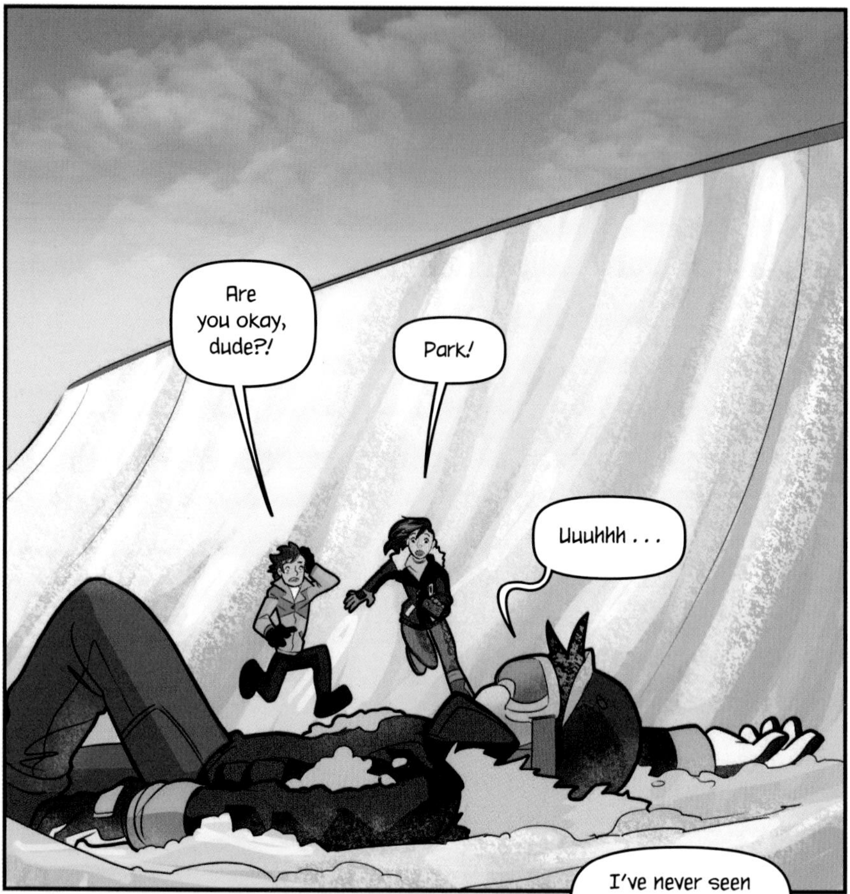
Are you okay, dude?!
Park!
Uuuhhh . . .

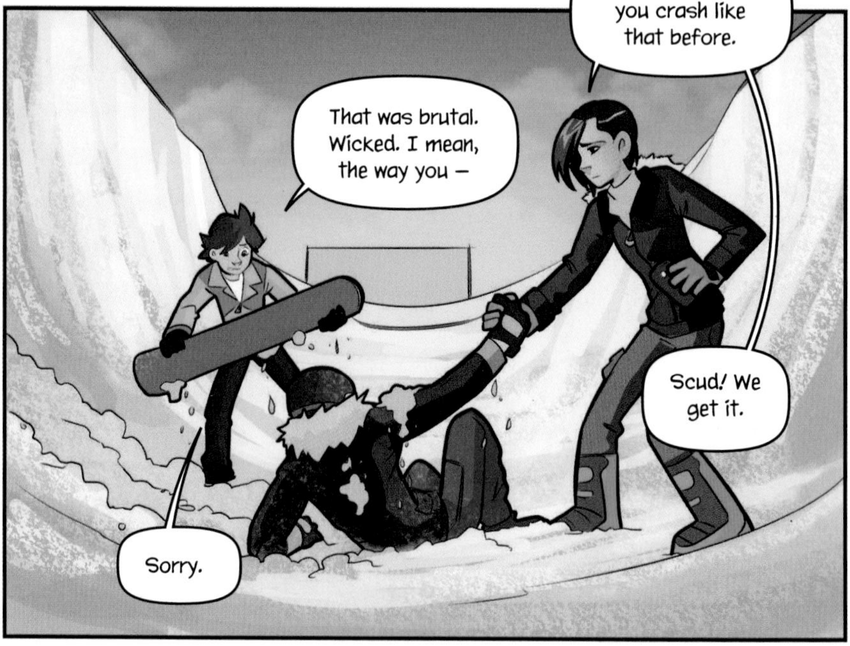
I've never seen you crash like that before.
That was brutal. Wicked. I mean, the way you —
Scud! We get it.
Sorry.

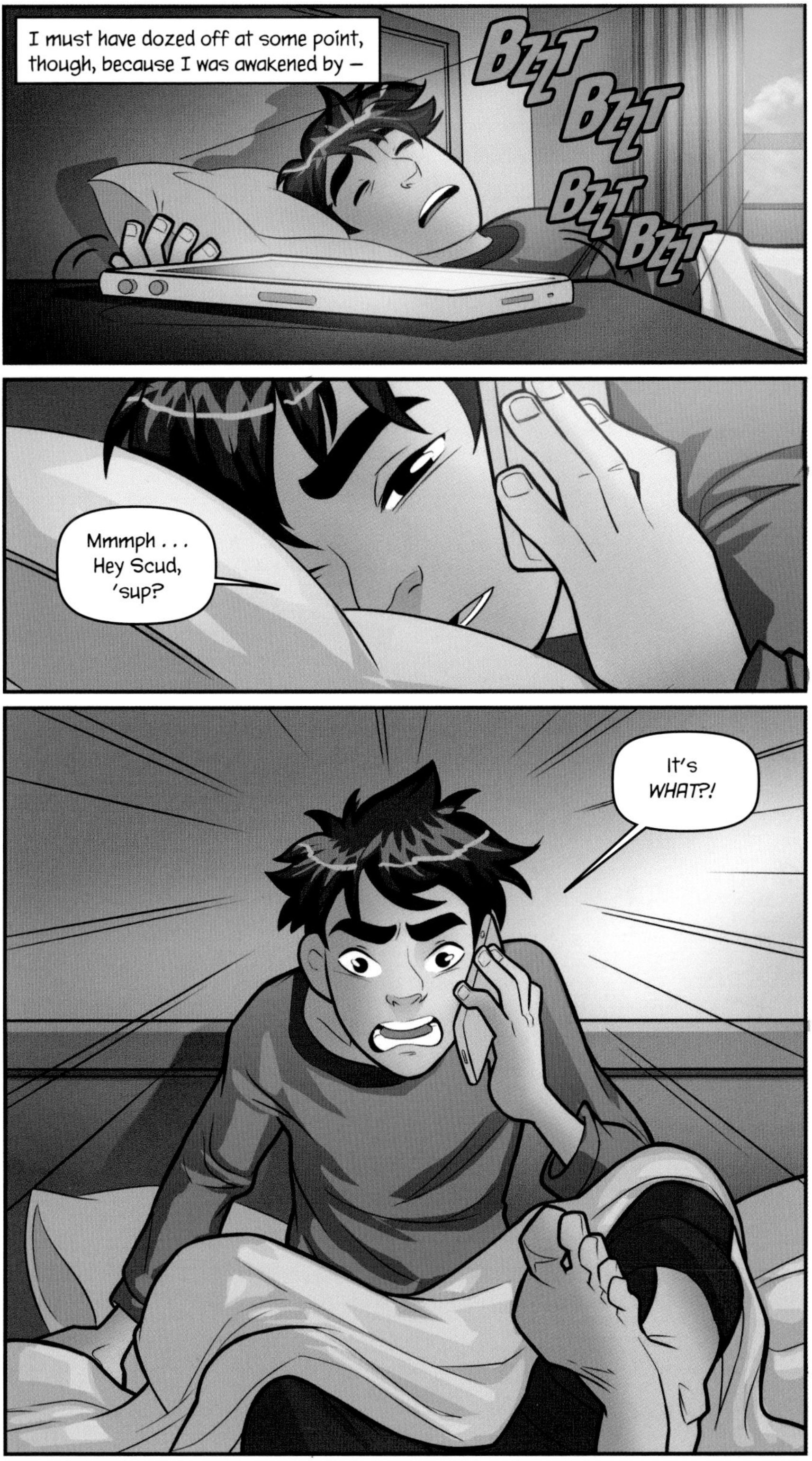
I must have dozed off at some point, though, because I was awakened by —
BZZT BZZT BZZT BZZT
Mmmph . . . Hey Scud, 'sup?
It's WHAT?!

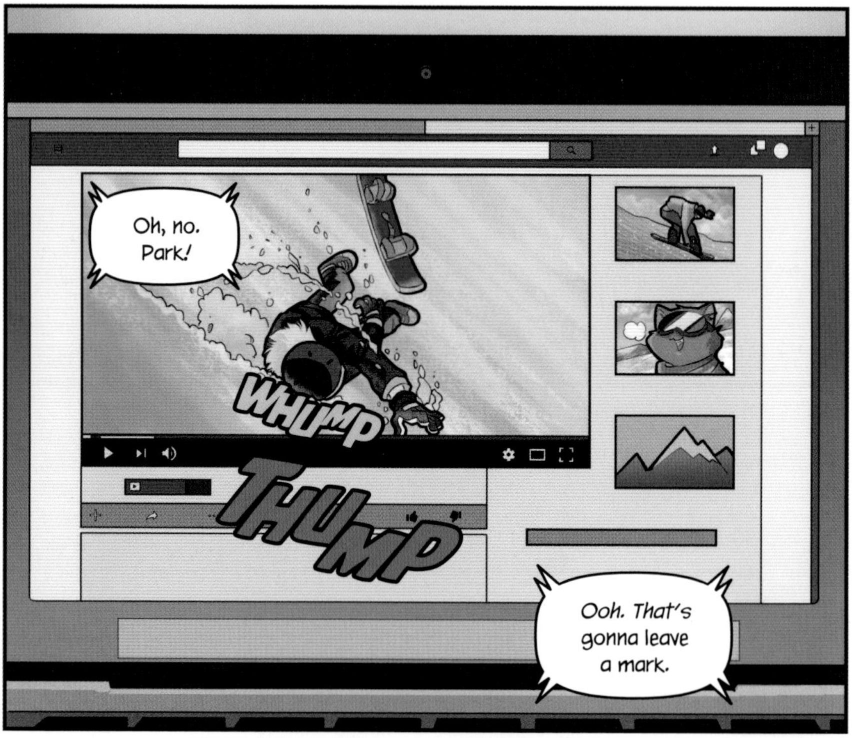
Oh, no.
Park!
WHUMP
THUMP
Ooh. That's gonna leave a mark.

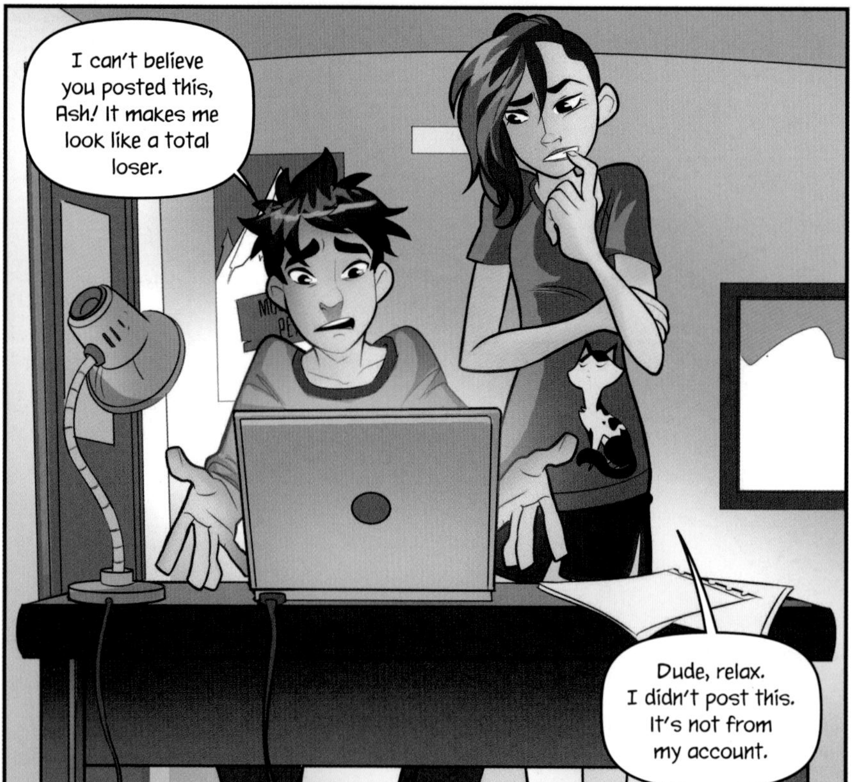
I can't believe you posted this, Ash! It makes me look like a total loser.
Dude, relax. I didn't post this. It's not from my account.

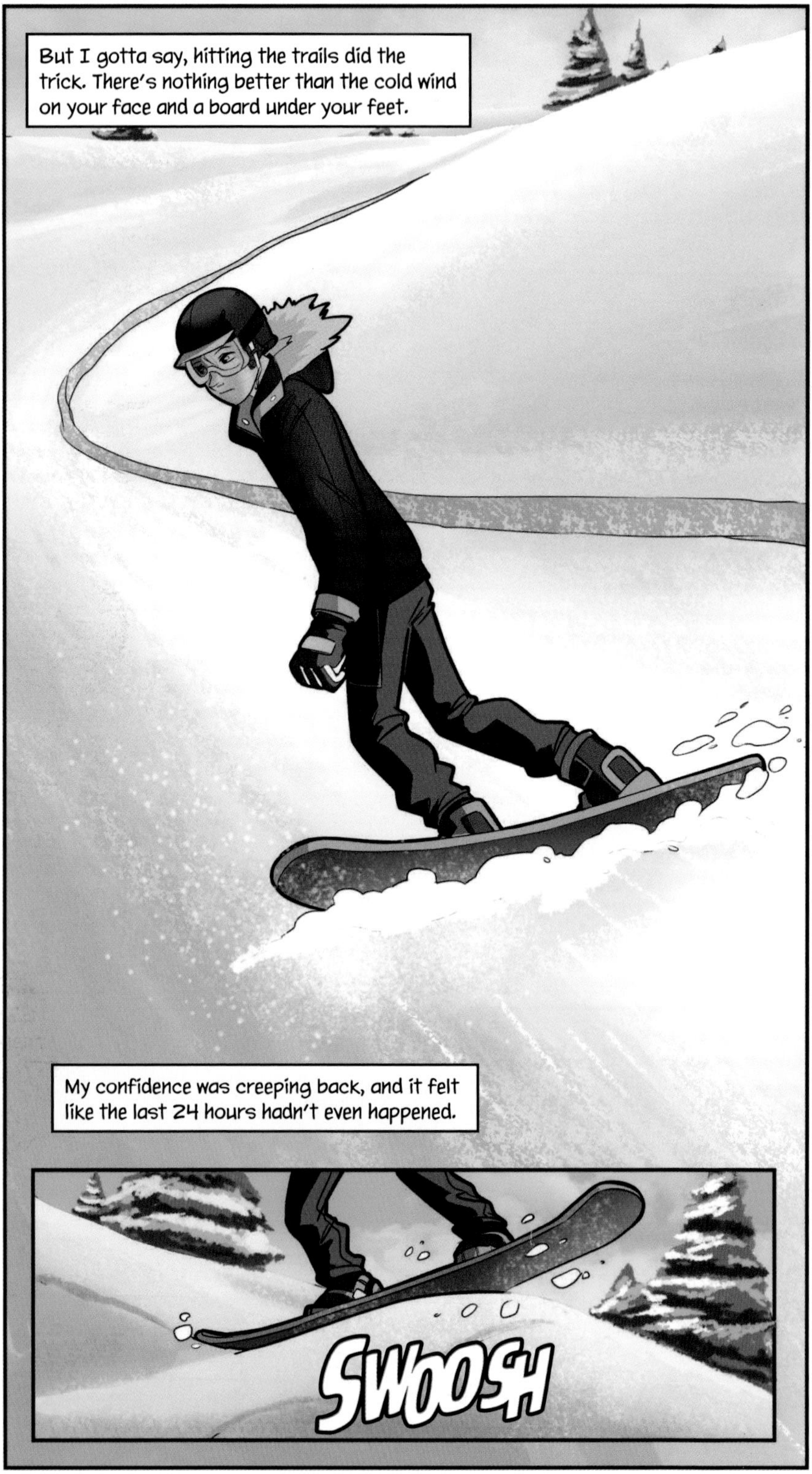
But I gotta say, hitting the trails did the trick. There's nothing better than the cold wind on your face and a board under your feet.
My confidence was creeping back, and it felt like the last 24 hours hadn't even happened.
SWOOSH

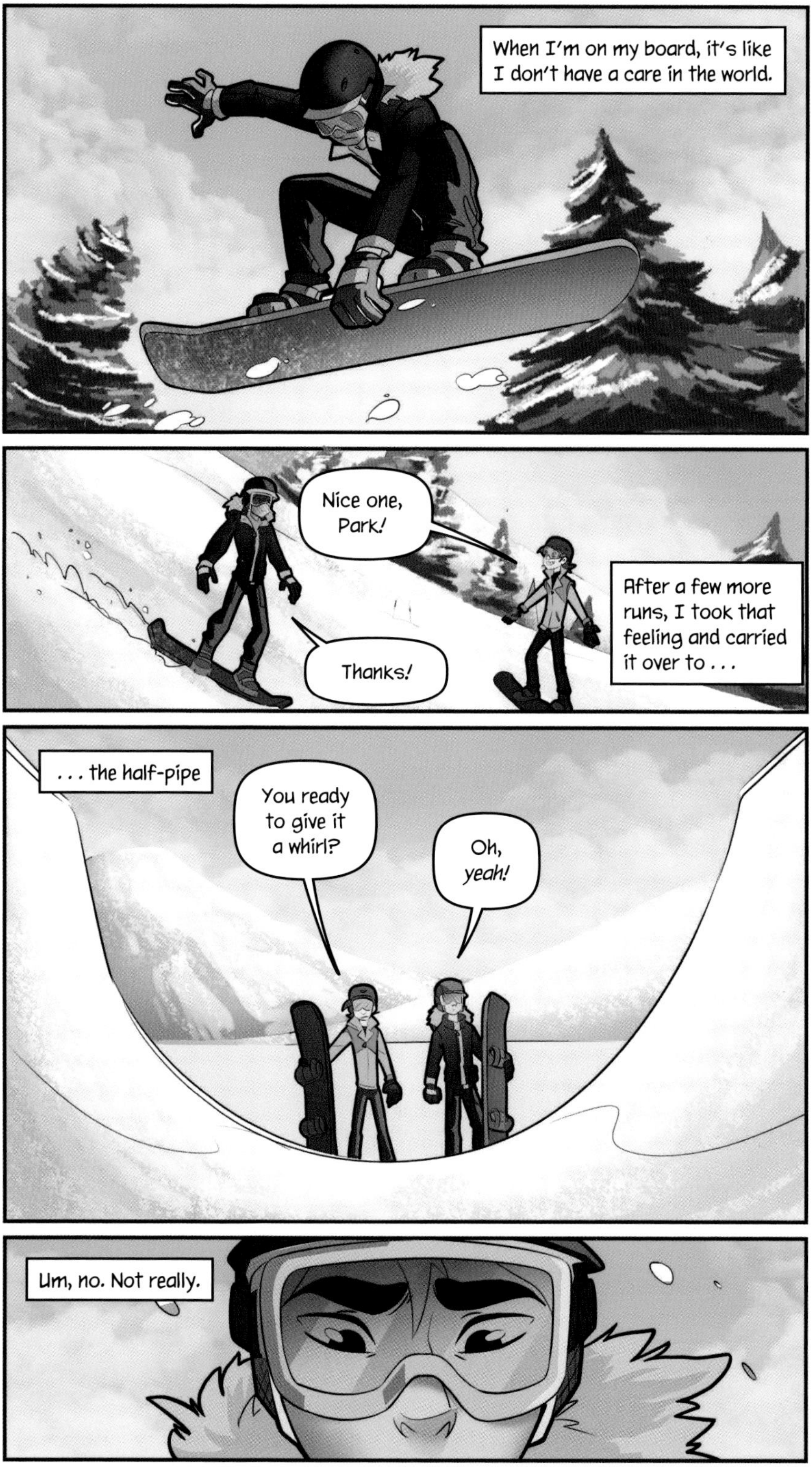
When I'm on my board, it's like I don't have a care in the world.
Nice one, Park!
Thanks!
After a few more runs, I took that feeling and carried it over to . . .
. . . the half-pipe
You ready to give it a whirl?
Oh, yeah!
Um, no. Not really.

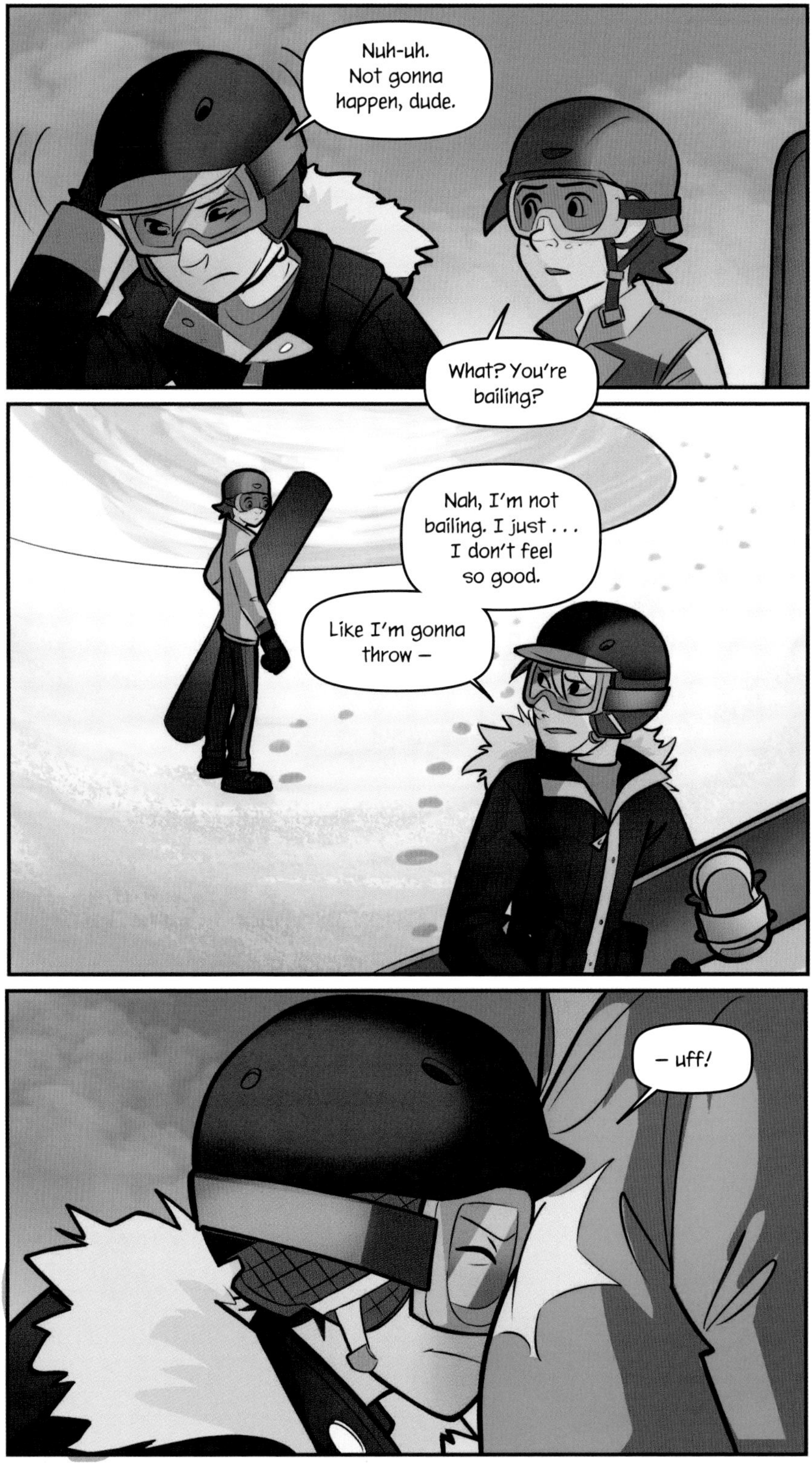
Nuh-uh. Not gonna happen, dude.
What? You're bailing?
Nah, I'm not bailing. I just . . . I don't feel so good.
Like I'm gonna throw –
– uff!

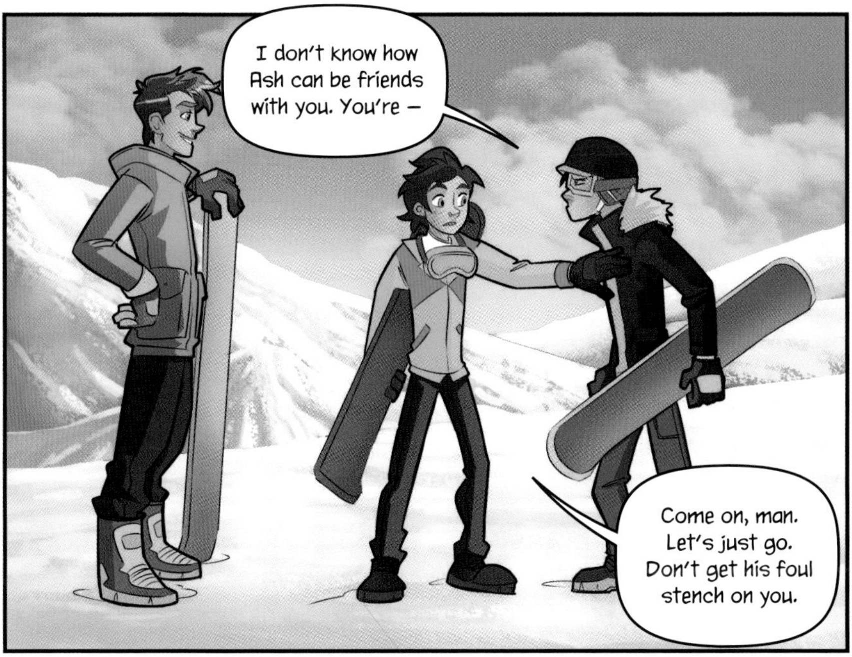
I don't know how Ash can be friends with you. You're —
Come on, man. Let's just go. Don't get his foul stench on you.

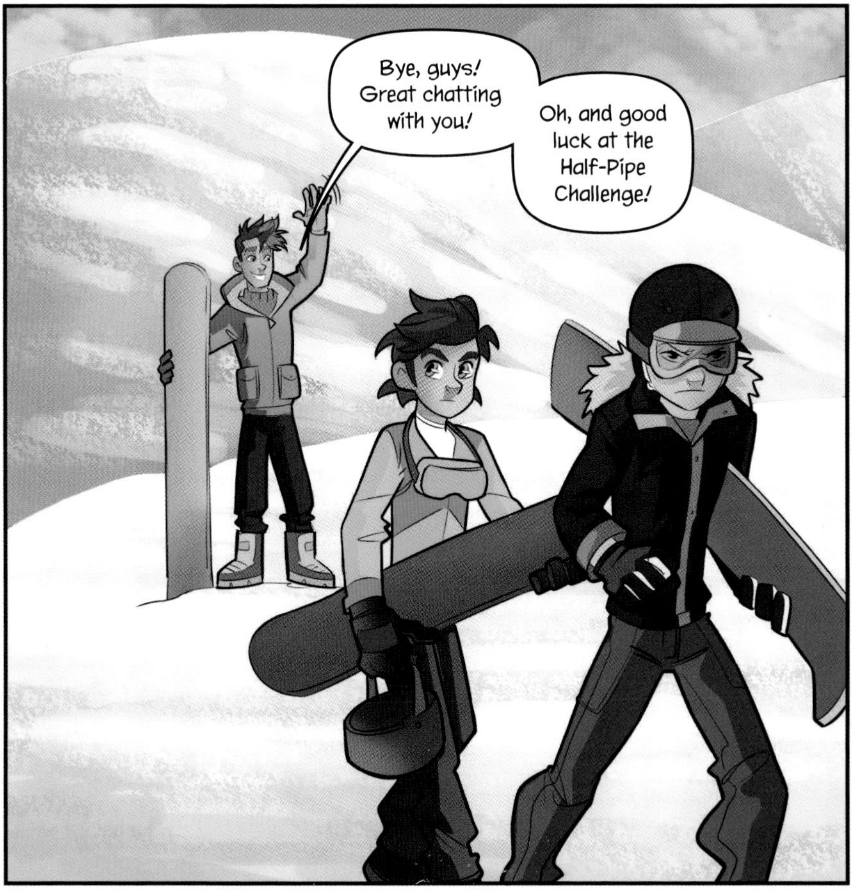
Bye, guys! Great chatting with you!
Oh, and good luck at the Half-Pipe Challenge!

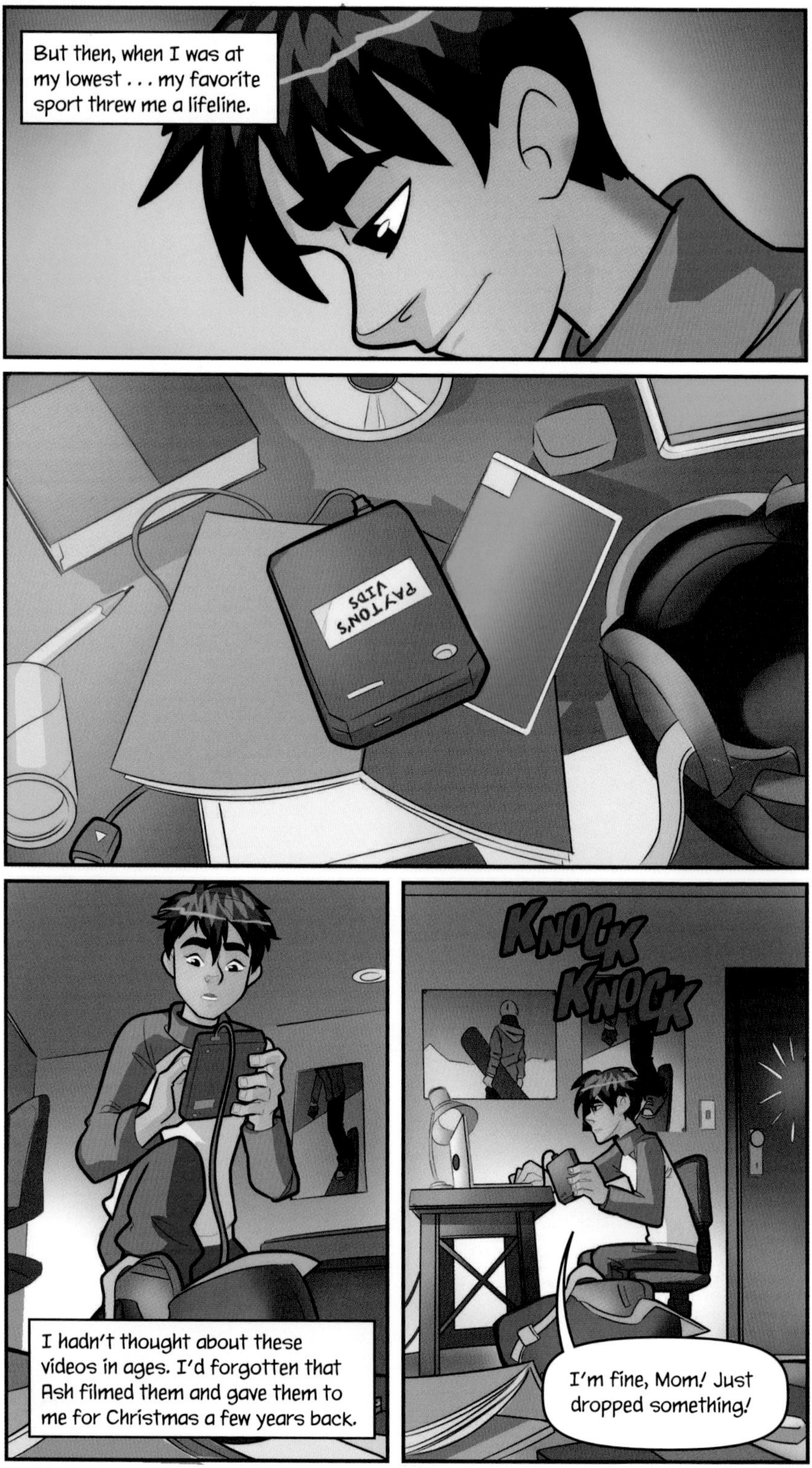
But then, when I was at my lowest . . . my favorite sport threw me a lifeline.
PAYTON'S VIDS
I hadn't thought about these videos in ages. I'd forgotten that Ash filmed them and gave them to me for Christmas a few years back.
KNOCK KNOCK
I'm fine, Mom! Just dropped something!

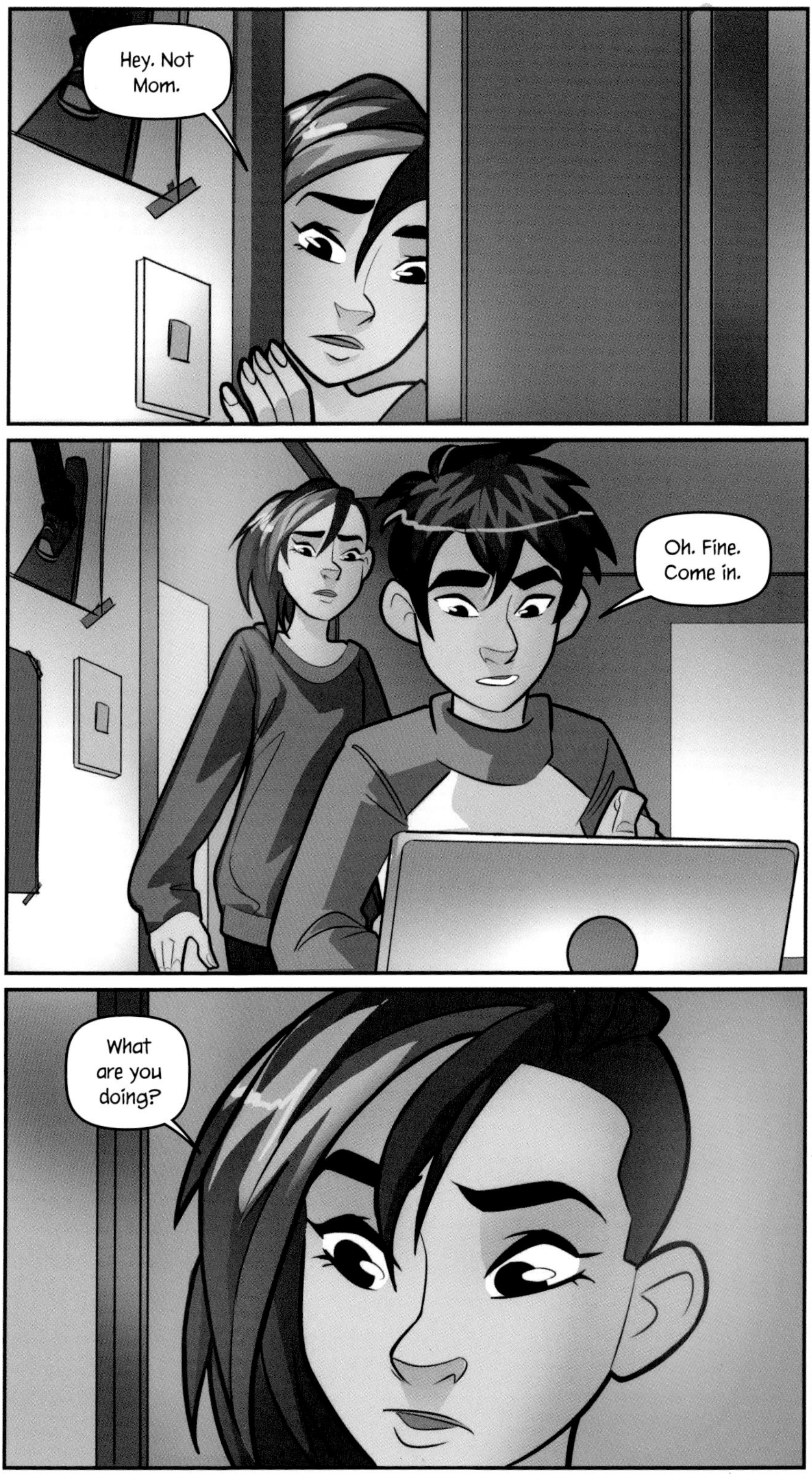
Hey. Not Mom.
Oh. Fine. Come in.
What are you doing?

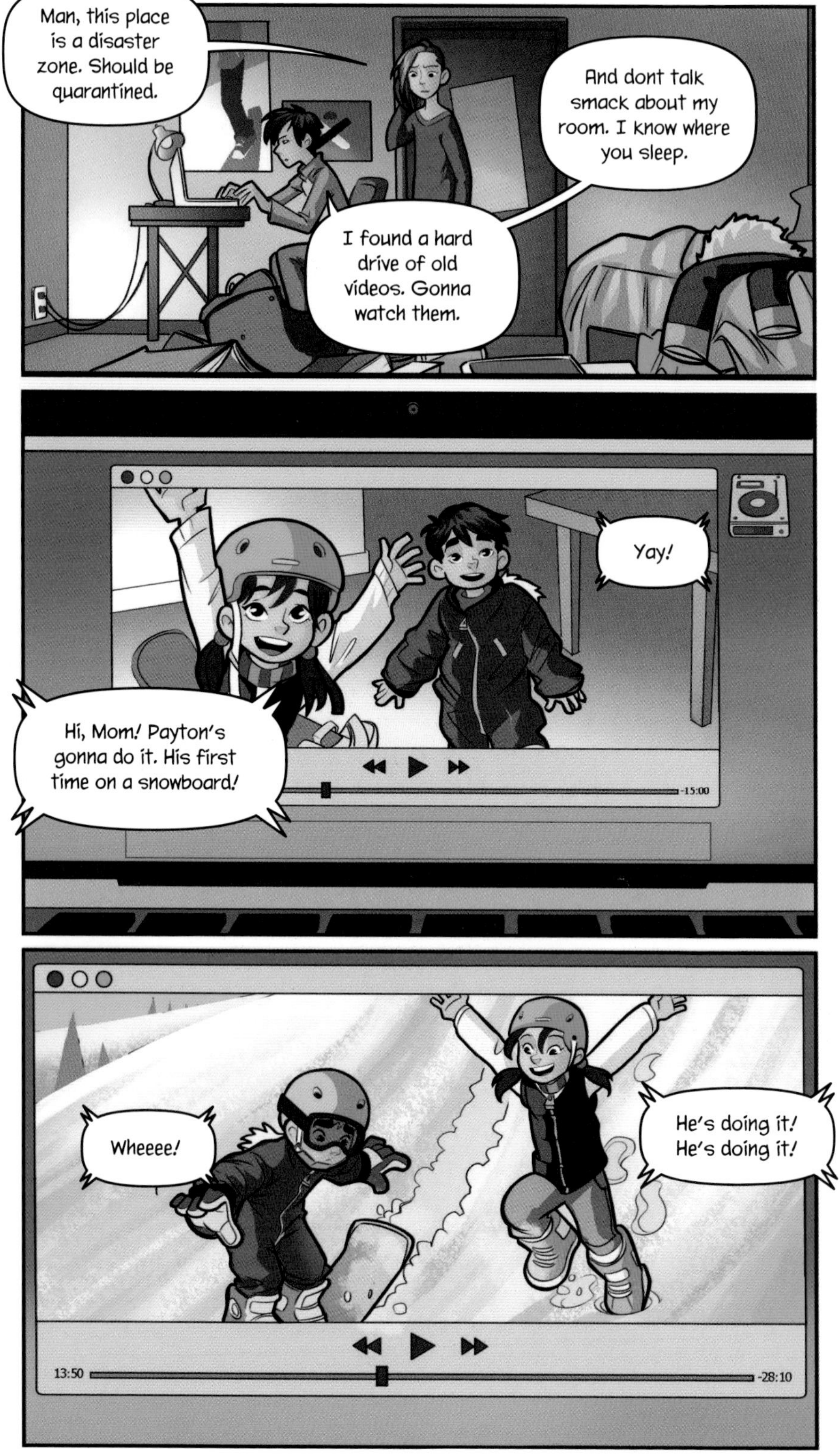
Man, this place is a disaster zone. Should be quarantined.
I found a hard drive of old videos. Gonna watch them.
And dont talk smack about my room. I know where you sleep.
Hi, Mom! Payton's gonna do it. His first time on a snowboard!
Yay!
-15:00
Wheeee!
He's doing it! He's doing it!
13:50
-28:10

The computer drive was full of videos showing me falling down and getting back up again.

09:40 -20:00

Ha, ha, ha!

12:35 -20:00

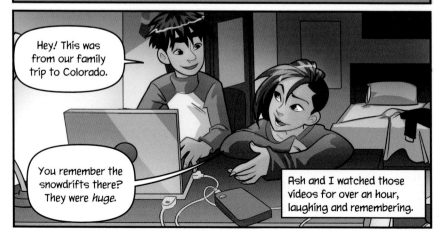

Hey! This was from our family trip to Colorado.

You remember the snowdrifts there? They were *huge.*

Ash and I watched those videos for over an hour, laughing and remembering.

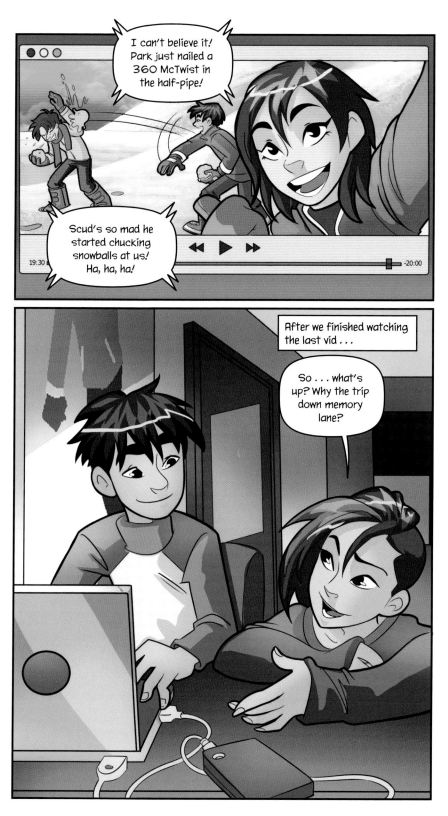

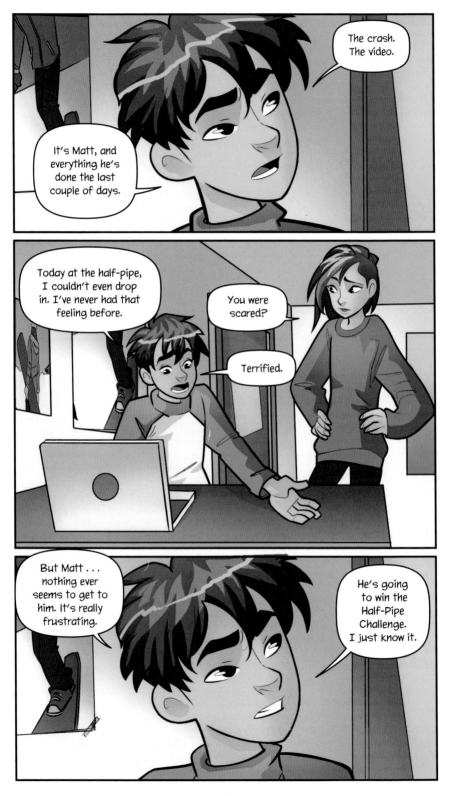

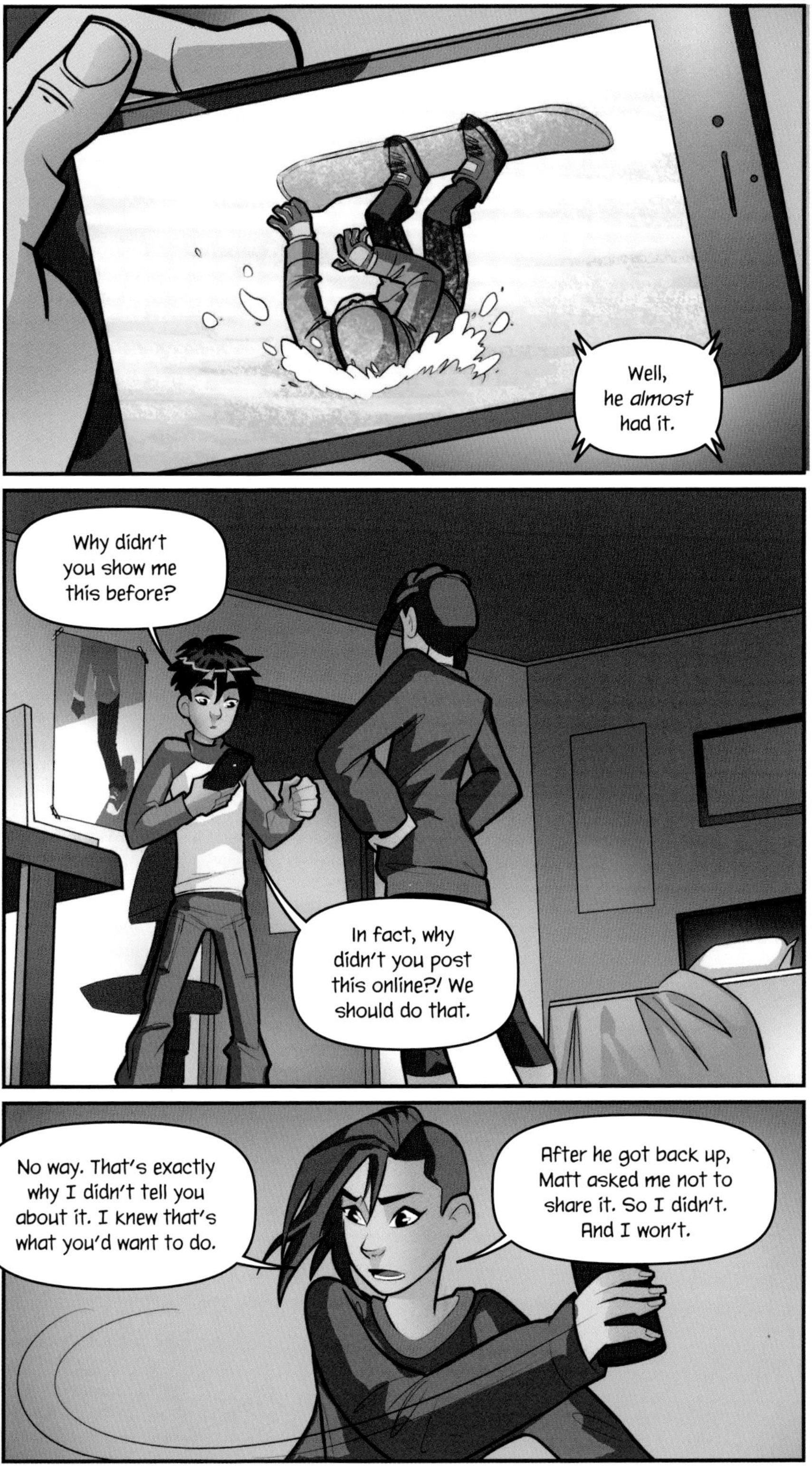
Well, he *almost* had it.
Why didn't you show me this before?
In fact, why didn't you post this online?! We should do that.
No way. That's exactly why I didn't tell you about it. I knew that's what you'd want to do.
After he got back up, Matt asked me not to share it. So I didn't. And I won't.

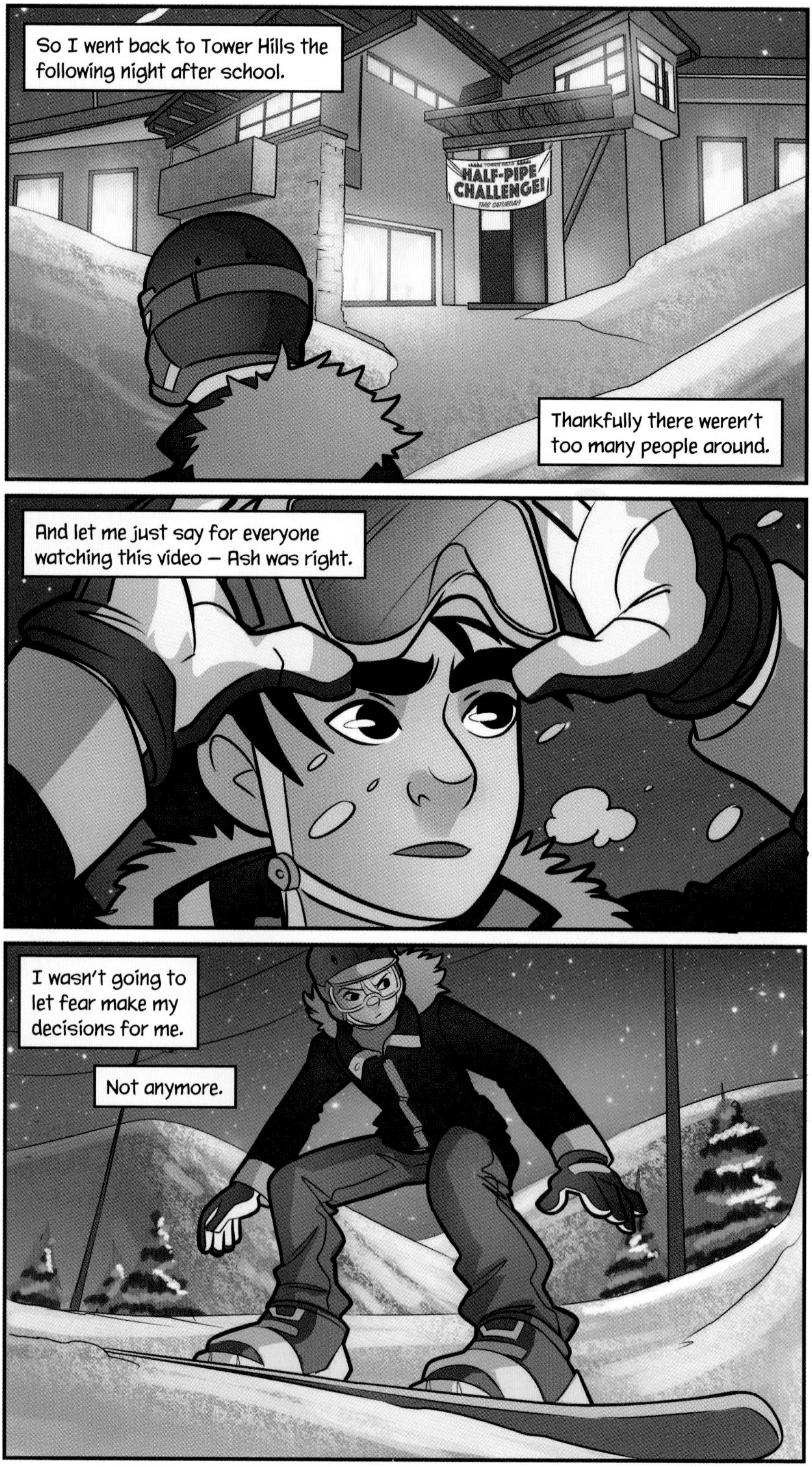
So I went back to Tower Hills the following night after school.
HALF-PIPE CHALLENGE!
Thankfully there weren't too many people around.
And let me just say for everyone watching this video — Ash was right.
I wasn't going to let fear make my decisions for me.
Not anymore.

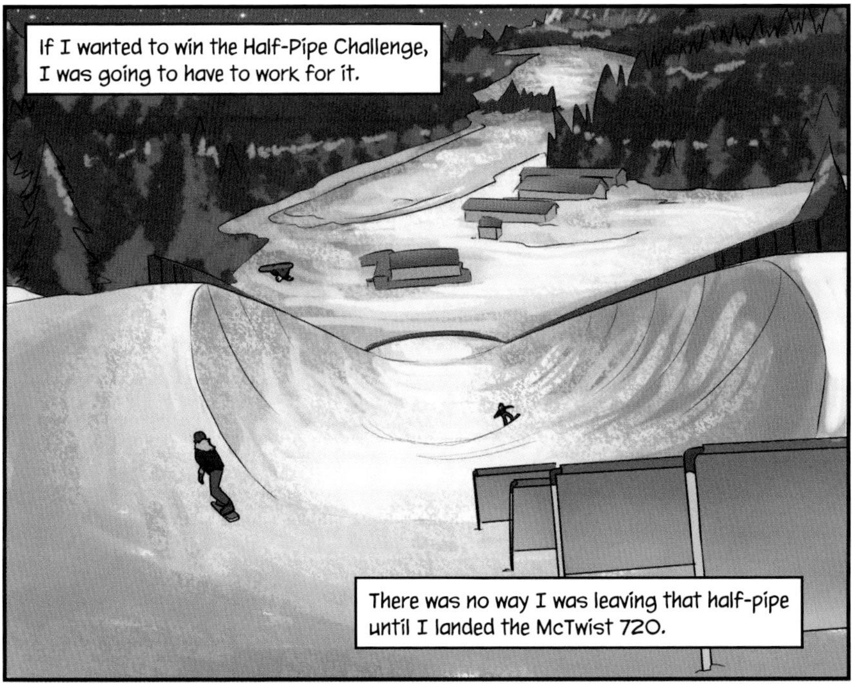
If I wanted to win the Half-Pipe Challenge, I was going to have to work for it.
There was no way I was leaving that half-pipe until I landed the McTwist 720.

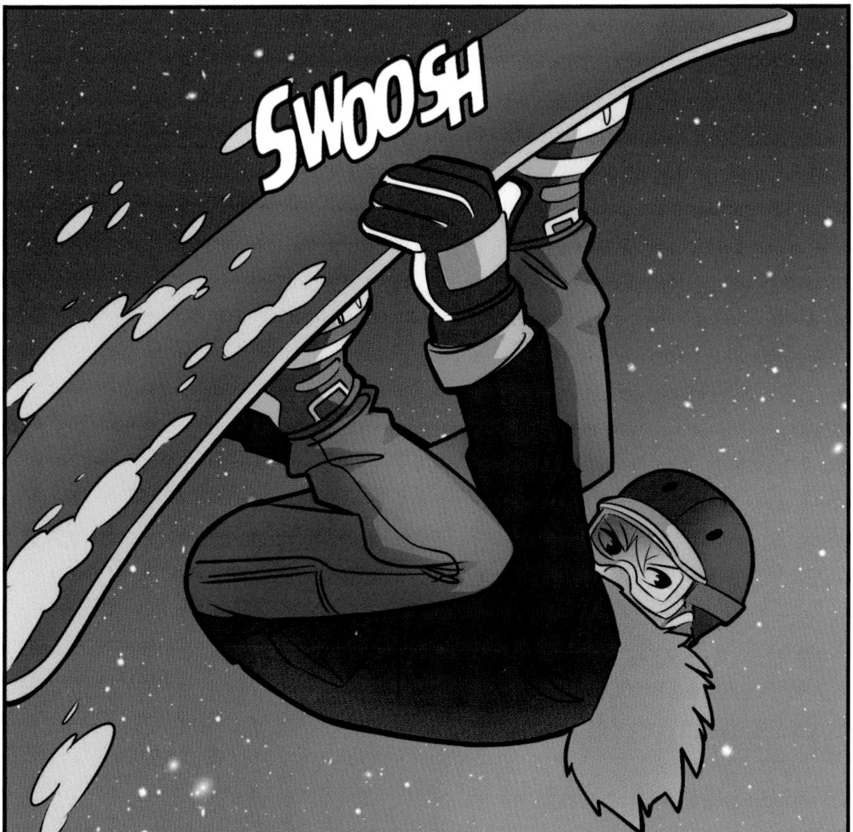
SWOOSH

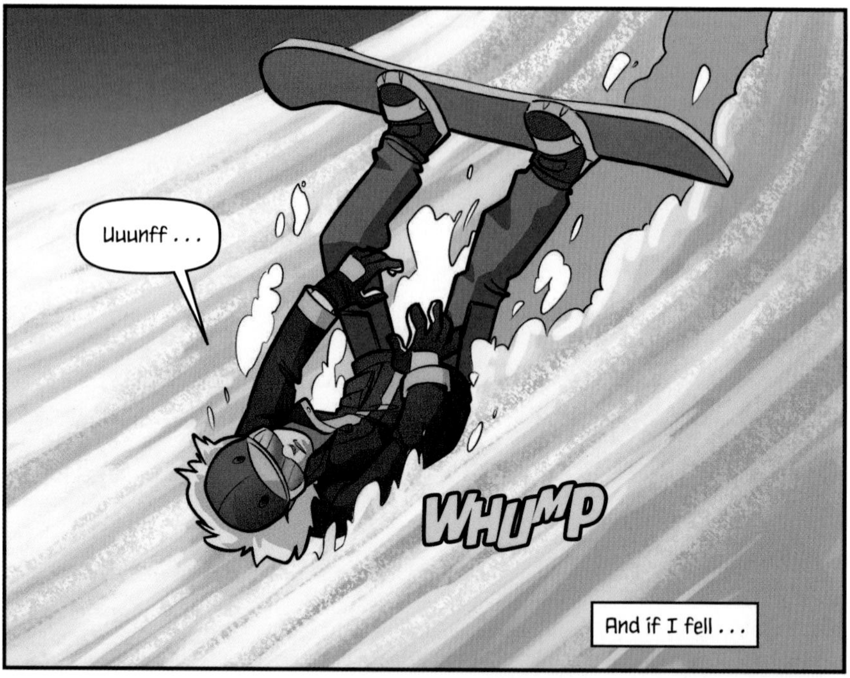
Uuunff . . .
WHUMP
And if I fell . . .

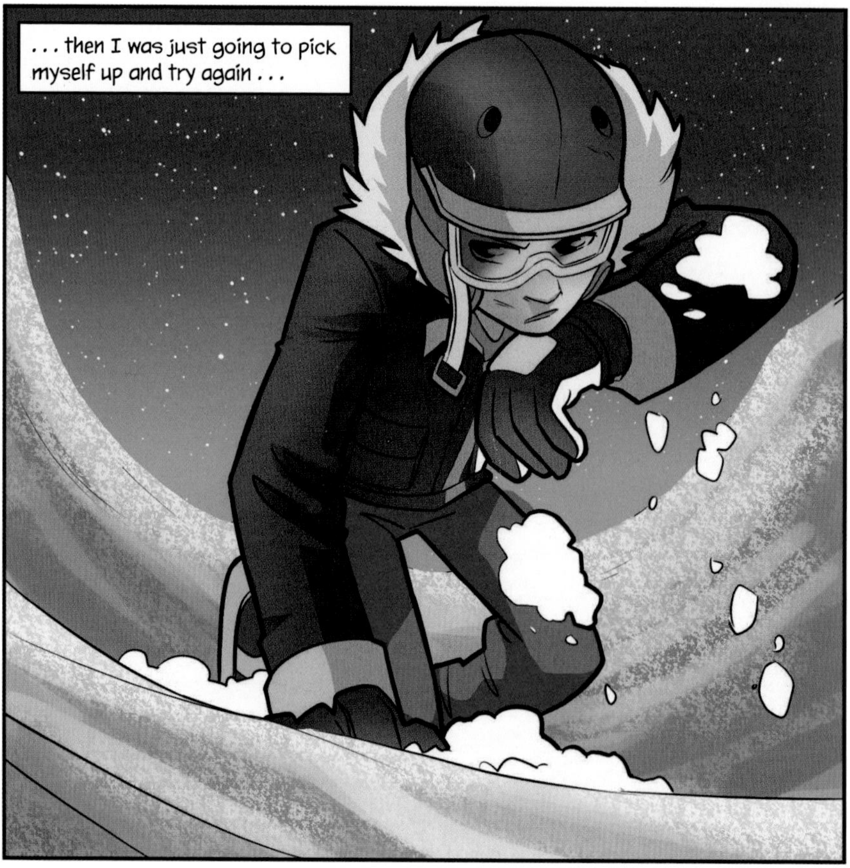
. . . then I was just going to pick myself up and try again . . .

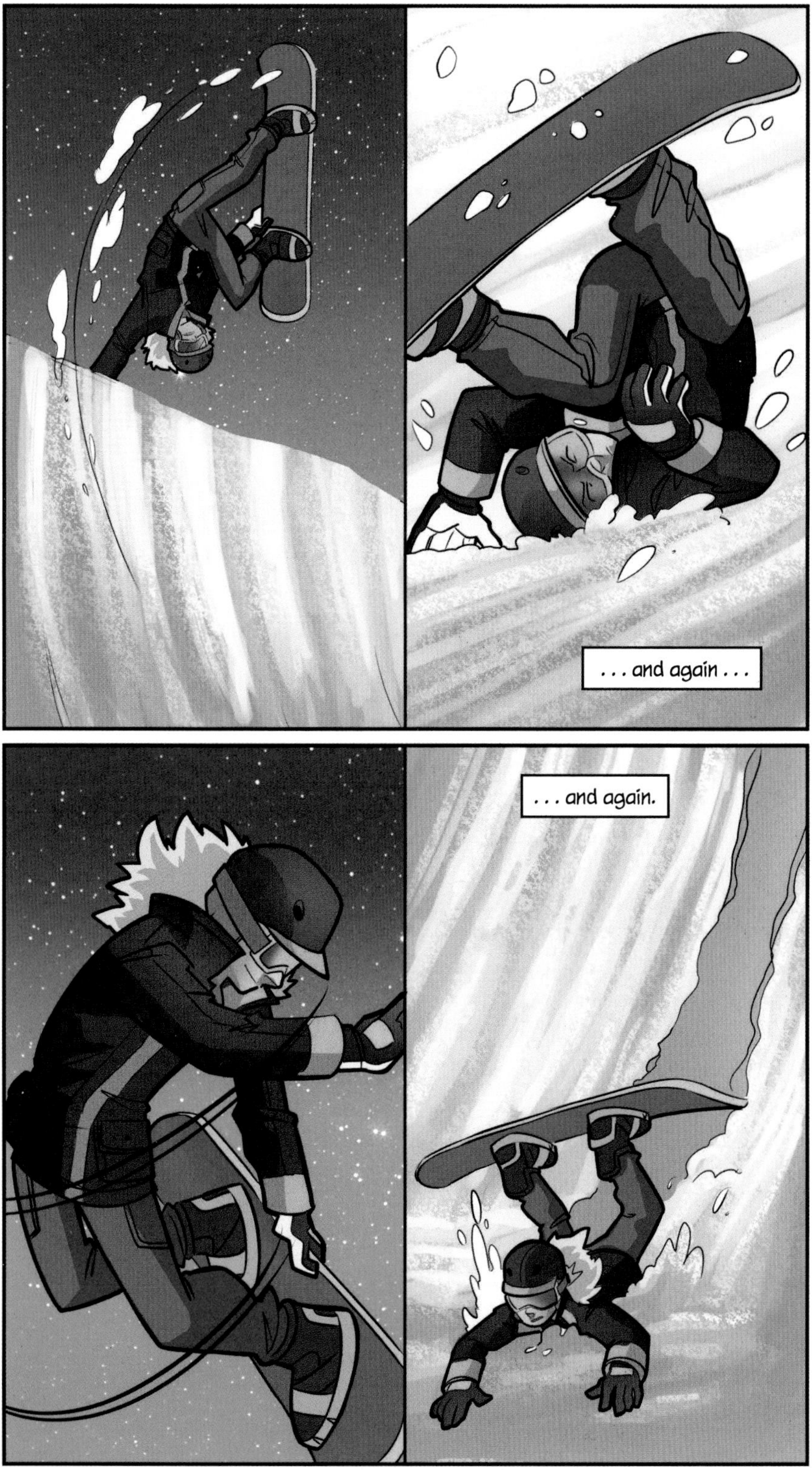
. . . and again . . .
. . . and again.

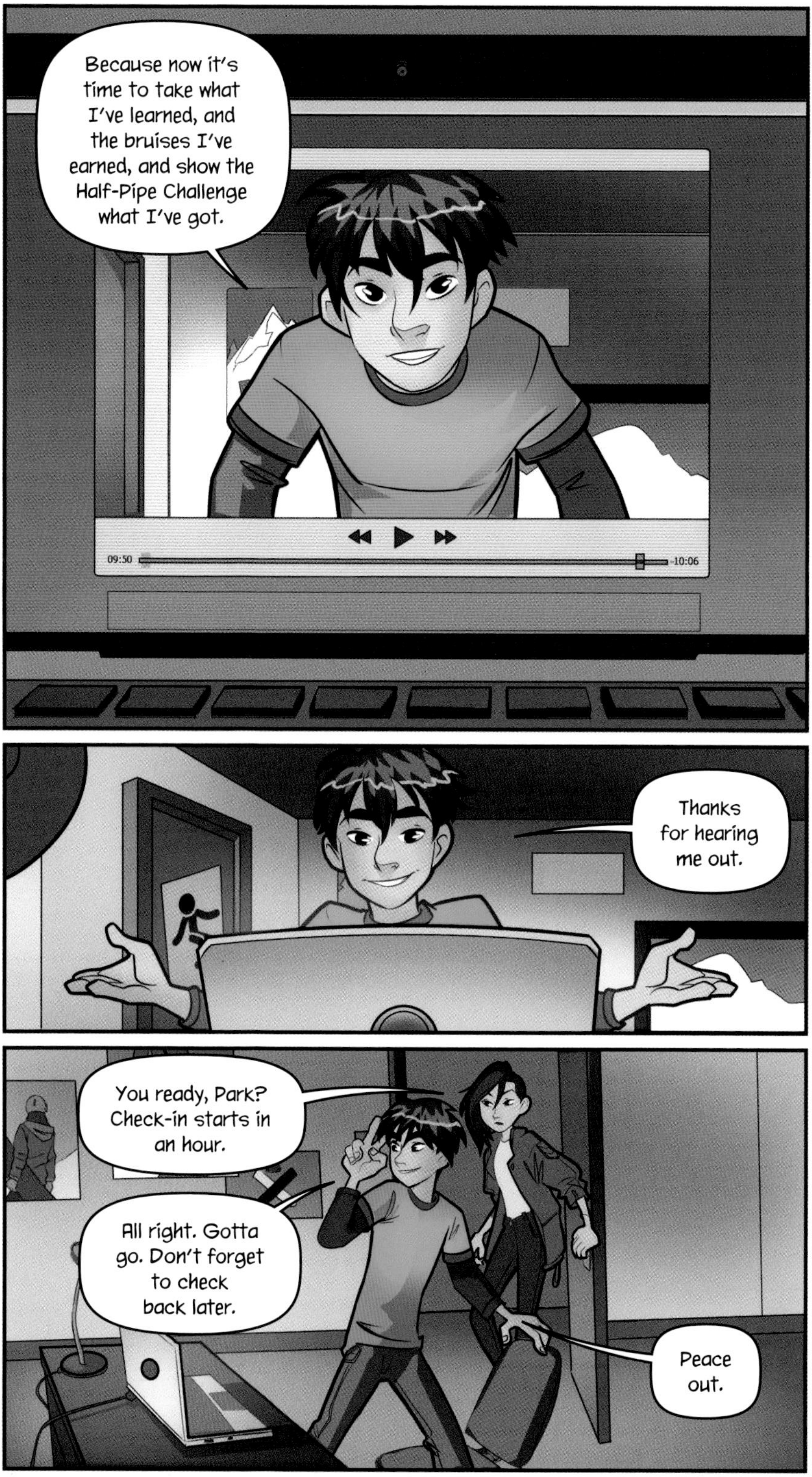
Because now it's time to take what I've learned, and the bruises I've earned, and show the Half-Pipe Challenge what I've got.
09:50
-10:06
Thanks for hearing me out.
You ready, Park? Check-in starts in an hour.
All right. Gotta go. Don't forget to check back later.
Peace out.

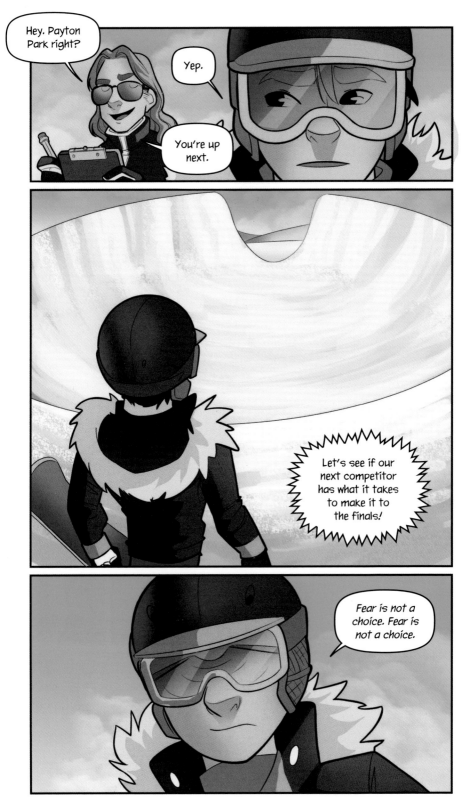

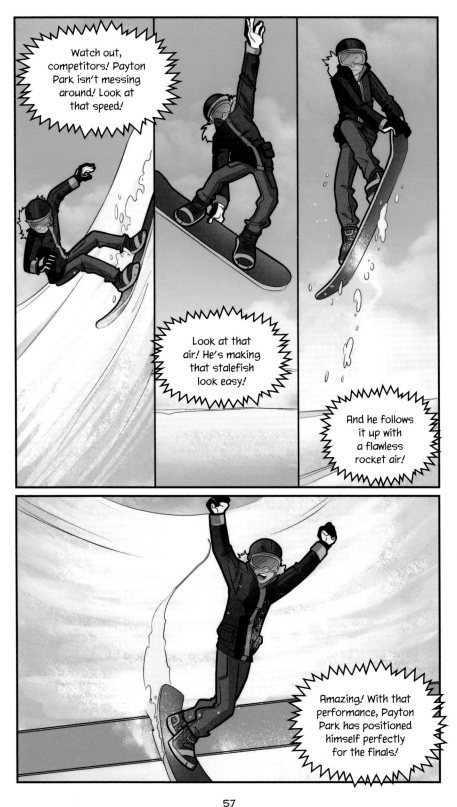

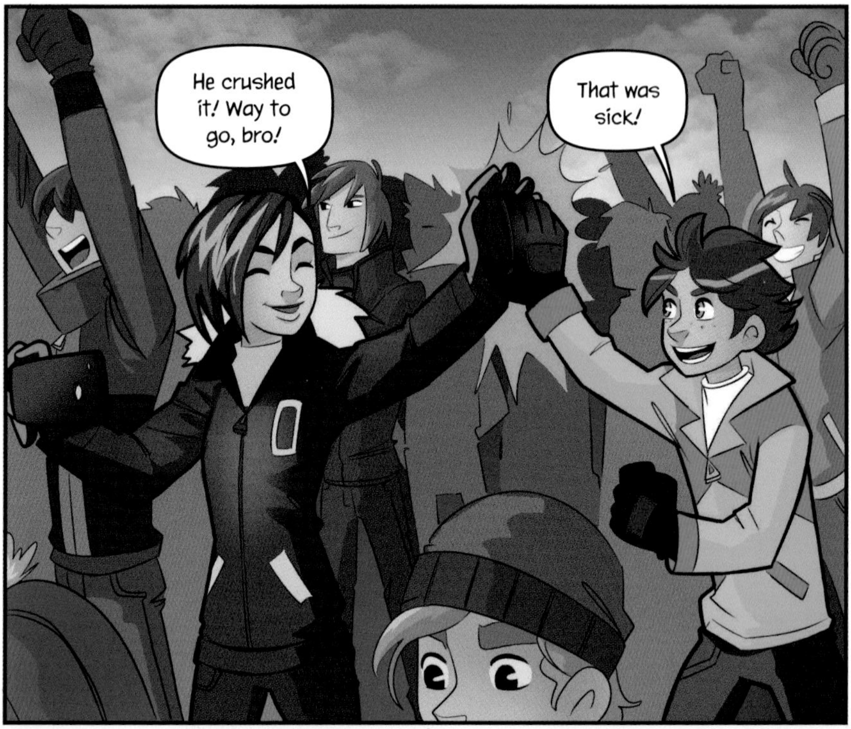
He crushed it! Way to go, bro!
That was sick!

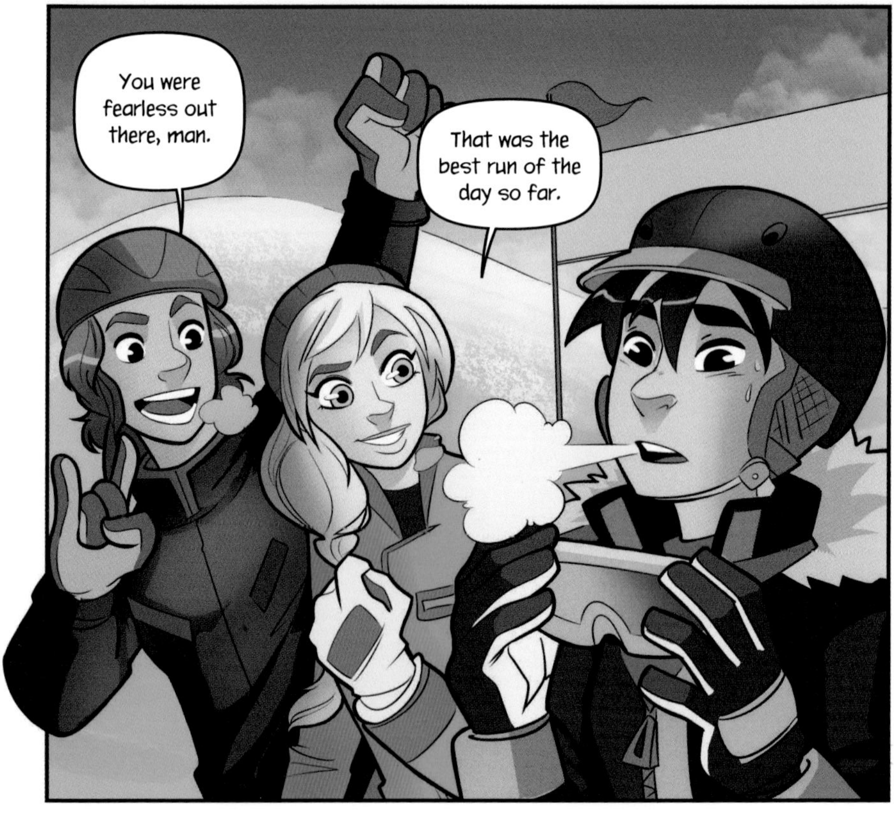
You were fearless out there, man.
That was the best run of the day so far.

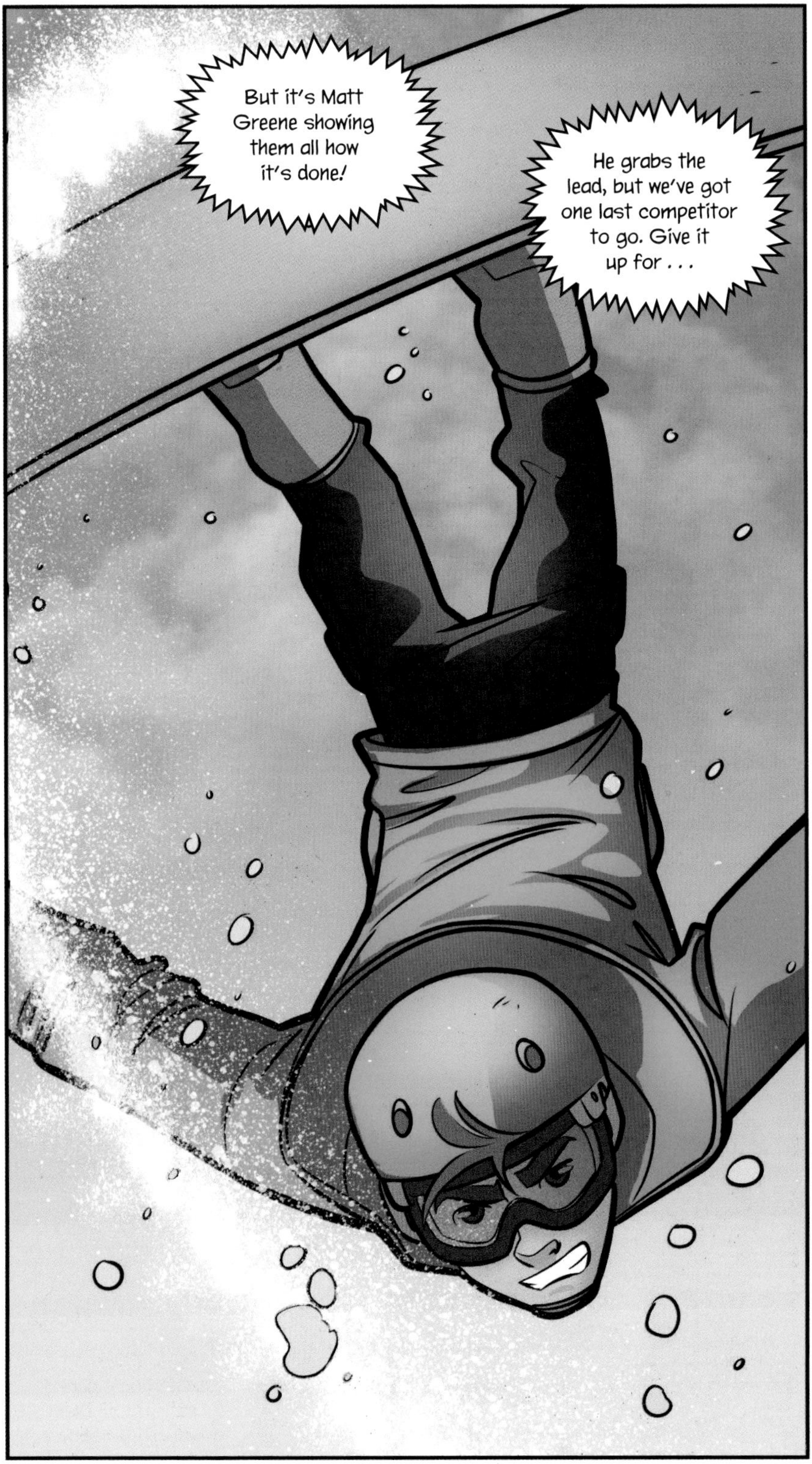
But it's Matt Greene showing them all how it's done!
He grabs the lead, but we've got one last competitor to go. Give it up for . . .

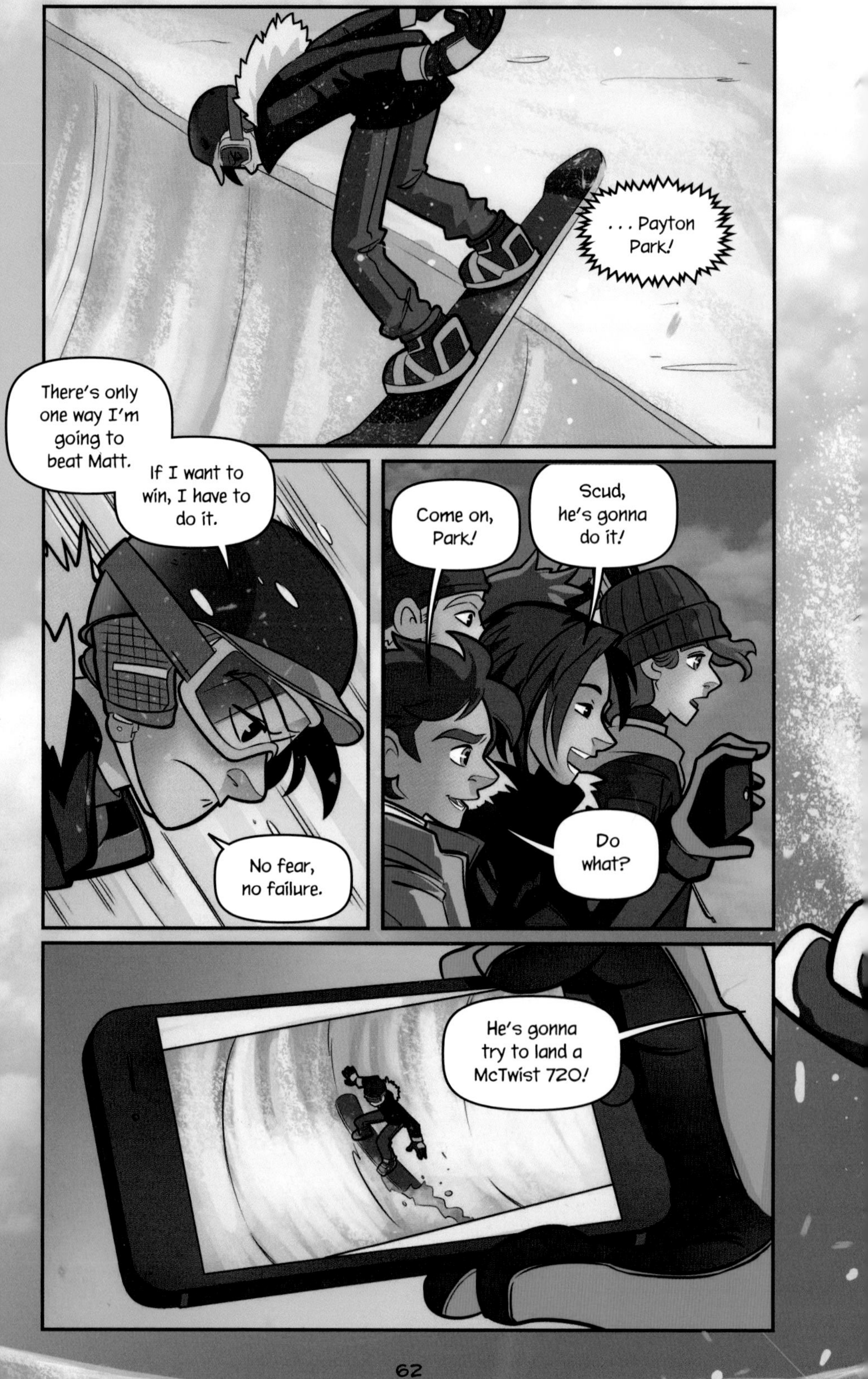
. . . Payton Park!
There's only one way I'm going to beat Matt.
If I want to win, I have to do it.
No fear, no failure.
Come on, Park!
Scud, he's gonna do it!
Do what?
He's gonna try to land a McTwist 720!

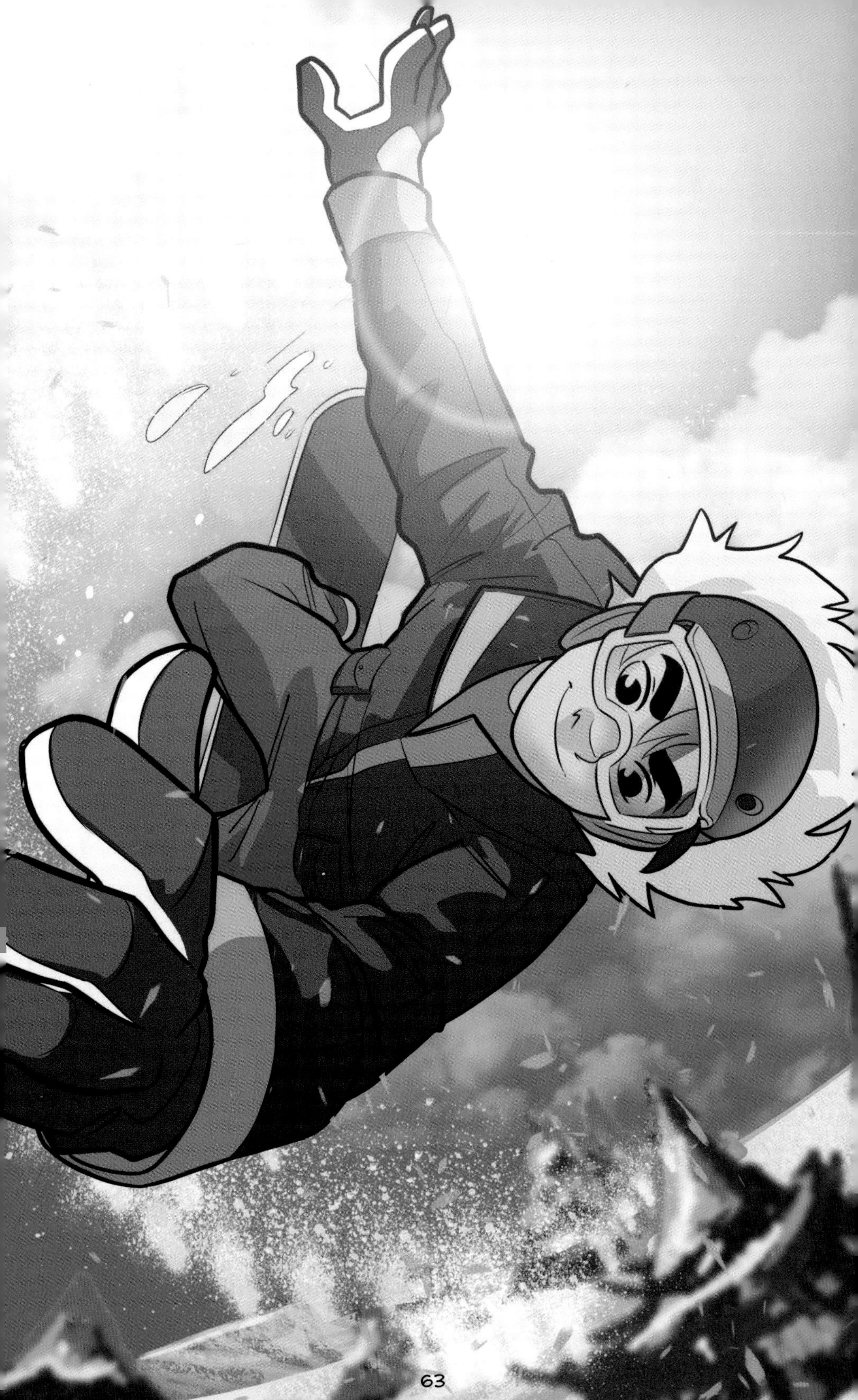

THE END

VISUAL QUESTIONS

1. Graphic novels use art to tell a story and to show us what a character is like. The above panel shows Park in his bedroom. What can we learn about him just by studying his room?

2. Closeups are a good way to show how someone is feeling during a story. Look at the above closeup panel. How do you think the character feels in this image?

3. Artists also use dramatic angles to help tell a story. Look at the panel below and describe how you think Park is feeling at this moment.

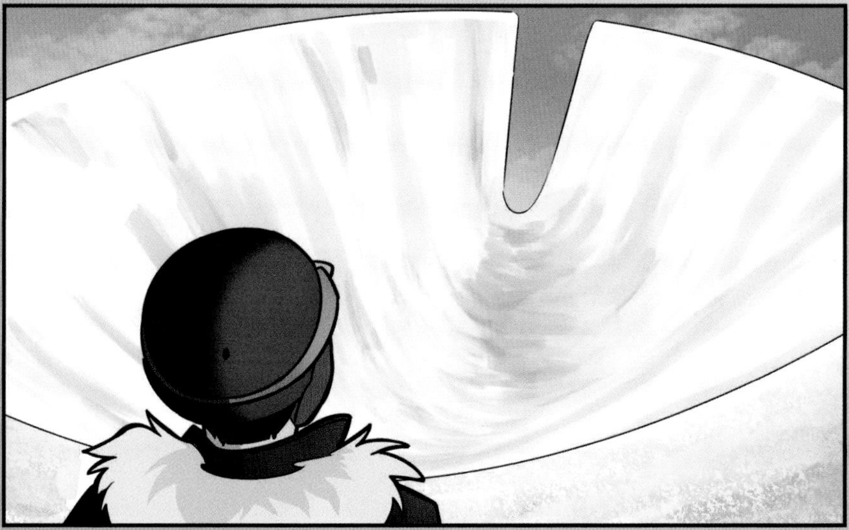

4. A series of panels can show several characters and scenes in a short amount of time to help keep the story moving. Look at the panels to the right. Can you tell what is happening in the story from the actions they show?

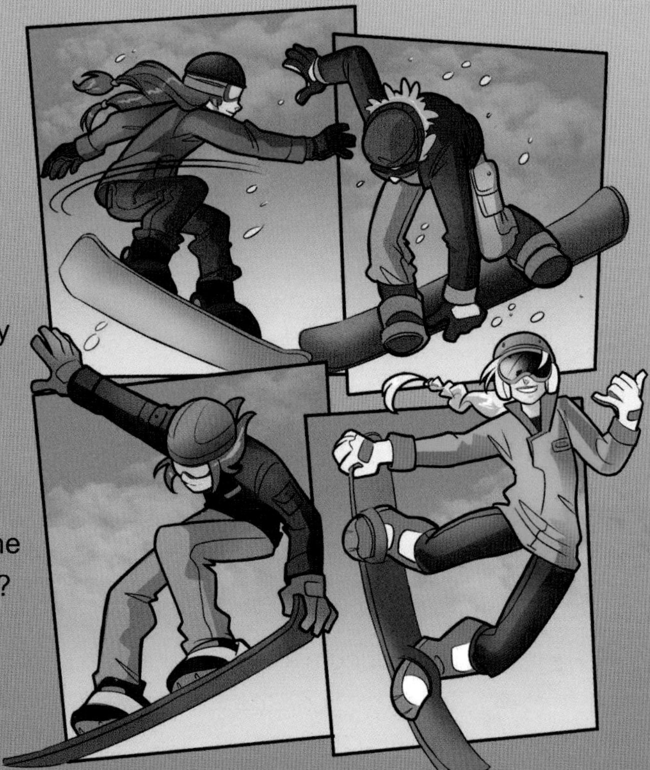

MORE ABOUT SNOWBOARDING

- Snowboarding is one of the most popular extreme sports in the world. It has been an Olympic event since 1998. The sport first debuted at the Nagano, Japan, Olympic Games that year.

- Snowboarding history is largely unknown. Many people credit M. J. Burchett from Utah with creating one of the first snowboards in 1929. He made it out of a plank of wood and used horse reins and clotheslines to secure his feet.

- The modern-day snowboard was invented in 1965 by Sherman Poppen. He wanted to create something that resembled surfing on snow. He bound two skis together into a "surf-type snow ski." Poppen originally called his device the "snurfer."

- There are several types of snowboarding events. Here are just a few:
  - In HALF-PIPE events boarders compete on a U-shaped ramp dug deep into a hill. Competitors rack up points by doing jumps, tricks, and twists.
  - SNOWBOARD CROSS is a speed competition that challenges riders to navigate through winding courses with narrow turns, jumps, berms, inclines, and drops.
  - SLOPESTYLE events are fast and wild! The courses are often covered with obstacles called "boxes" that look like big, slippery tabletops. Another obstacle often seen is the rail.

- Shaun White is one of the world's greatest boarders. He has won two Olympic gold medals in snowboarding. He's also won an amazing 24 combined medals in the Winter and Summer X Games in various snowboard and skateboard events.

SNOWBOARD TRICK GLOSSARY

360 — A trick involving one full spin while in the air.

540 — A trick involving one and one half spins while in the air.

720 — A trick involving two full spins while in the air.

BACKSIDE — When a rider spins in a clockwise direction during a trick.

FRONTSIDE — When a rider spins in a counter-clockwise direction during a trick.

METHOD AIR — A trick in which a rider bends both knees and grabs the heel edge of the board to pull it level with his or her head.

MCTWIST — A complicated trick in which a rider performs a backside 540 while doing a front flip and then lands riding forward.

MUTE AIR — A trick in which the rider grabs the toe edge of the board either between the toes or in front of the front foot.

ROCKET AIR — A trick in which the rider grabs the toe edge of the board closest to the front foot while it points toward the ground.

RODEO FLIP — A trick in which the rider performs a 540 spin while doing a frontward or backward flip at the same time.

STALEFISH — A trick in which the rider grabs the heel edge of the board between the bindings next to the rear foot.

TAILGRAB — A trick in which the rider grabs the tail end of the board while in the air.

GLOSSARY

chalet (sha-LAY)—a house or building on a mountain often used by skiers and snowboarders to rest and get warm

coping (KOH-ping)—the top edge of a half-pipe ramp

half-pipe (HAF-pipe)—a U-shaped ramp with high walls

humiliate (hyoo-MIL-ee-ate)—to make someone look or feel foolish or embarrassed

inferno (in-FUR-noh)—an intense fire

quarantine (KWOR-uhn-teen)—to keep people or animals separated to stop the spread of disease

social media (SOH-shuhl MEE-dee-uh)—forms of electronic communication, such as websites and online blogs, in which users share information, ideas, personal messages, and other content

withdraw (with-DRAW)—to remove oneself from participation in a competition

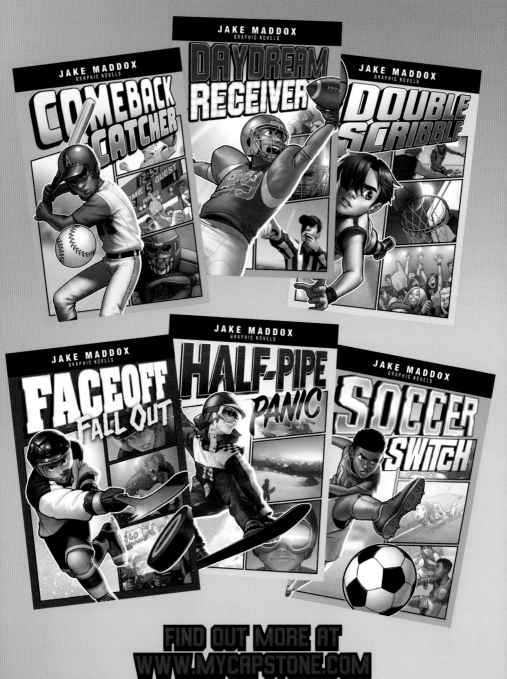

ABOUT THE AUTHOR

Brandon Terrell is the author of numerous children's books, including several volumes in both the Tony Hawk 900 Revolution series and the Tony Hawk Live2Skate series. He has also written several Spine Shivers titles, and is the author of the Sports Illustrated Kids: Time Machine Magazine series. When not hunched over his laptop, Brandon enjoys watching movies and TV, reading, watching and playing baseball, and spending time with his wife and two children at his home in Minnesota.

ABOUT THE ARTISTS

Berenice Muñiz is a Mexican artist from Monterrey. She has been drawing and coloring comics since 2009. Her work can be found on several children's books in her country, where she lives with her beloved partner in crime, a shaggy dog and four cats.

Nephtali Leal is a Mexican artist from Monterrey. His skills have helped him land work on comics, video games, animations, and production centers. Nep's a cinema enthusiast and he has worked on several areas such as VFX, FX motion graphics storyboarding, concept art, and more.

Jaymes Reed has operated the company Digital-CAPS: Comic Book Lettering since 2003. He has done lettering for many publishers, most notably and recently Avatar Press. He's also the only letterer working with Inception Strategies, an Aboriginal-Australian publisher that develops social comics with public service messages for the Australian government. Jaymes is also a 2012 and 2013 Shel Dorf Award Nominee.